M

My Year in Agony

Miss
Understanding
She tells it like it is

My Year
in Agony

Hodder
Children's
Books

A division of Hachette Children's Books

Copyright © 2009 T. S. Easton

First published in Great Britain in 2009
by Hodder Children's Books

The right of T. S. Easton to be identified as the Author of
the Work has been asserted by her in accordance with the
Copyright, Designs and Patents Act 1988

1

A Catalogue record for this book is available from the British Library

ISBN 978 0 340 98882 4

Typeset in Berkeley by Avon DataSet Ltd,
Bidford on Avon, Warwickshire

Printed in the UK by CPI Bookmarque, Croydon, CR0 4TD

The paper and board used in this paperback by Hodder Children's Books
are natural recyclable products made from wood grown in
sustainable forests. The manufacturing processes conform to the
environmental regulations of the country of origin.

Hodder Children's Books
A division of Hachette Children's Books
338 Euston Road, London NW1 3BH
An Hachette UK company

For Flemingc

Miss Understanding Blog Entry
– 1st October 2009

Hey there you.

Well, I'm back everyone! After two weeks' break, in which I was taken by my grandparents and brought to their cottage in Devon.

First of all, I must make it clear that I like Devon, even the flooded bits. And I love Granny and Gramps, even though they've become overly reliant on Werther's Originals. And my brother and I spend many happy evenings helping them file junk mail they've received from companies trying to sell them cruises or stair-lifts. Or sometimes cruises *with* stair-lifts. Good times.

But I'm totally hacked off with my mother. I may have bored you with this before, but she is always trying to get out of 'kid duty' and happily palms my little brother and me off on any random adult. Luckily my grandparents are sane and humane people who understand the meaning of adult responsibility and seem to like spending time with us, their grandchildren. But Mum's second adolescence – or third, if you listen to my dad – is starting to get on everyone's nerves. I definitely noticed mild-mannered granny rolling her eyes at the kaftan-and-clogs ensemble Mum was wearing when she dropped us off; even Marley has started asking why Mummy looks like Dobby the House Elf. My mother obviously wants us out of the house so that she can have a week of Ashtanga yoga sessions and meditate in peace without me playing The Cold War Kids with the bass right up and Marley using her Peace Pyramid as a fort. We bring on her migraines, apparently.

Anyway, teenage whine over for now. I hope you like the new-look page. As you'll have noticed, my advice column is no longer hosted by the school's website. They threw me off whilst I was away.

I can only think it was because in my last column I passed comment on the fact Ms Chilton had a VPL at the Meet-the-Teacher evening last month. Don't shoot the messenger, OK? I only mentioned it so that she'd know for next time. Honestly, you try to do someone a favour . . .

But if I'm being honest, the school website and I have been going through some difficulties lately.

I said, 'How about a trial separation?'

They said, 'Error 401 – access denied.'

I'm OK about it. To be honest I felt *oppressed, repressed,* and *depressed* by the attempts to censor my column; they said I was 'subversive and flippant, and a bad influence on the pupils of Adam Woodyatt Academy'. Whatevs. Listen, school's a good thing, honestly it is, and the teachers all care and stuff . . . But jeez Louise, have they not heard of the freedom of speech?

Anyway, to cut a long story marginally shorter, I've gone solo, here at *Missunderstanding.net*, where I truly belong. Yep, not only can you read and write to me for advice, but Miss Understanding's blog is only a click away!

So welcome to the very first Miss Understanding's Advice Column and General Gossip Blog (snappy title pending). Loads of emails waiting for me when I got back. I'm flattered, and thanks for bringing me up to speed with what's been happening at school and this old town we call Allerton, Bucks.

To the person who emailed to say this was a bitchin' site, I trust you meant bitchin' as in fabulous, rather than bitchin' as in bitchy, cos we don't bitch here, do we? We just *observe*. Case in point – Ms Cooper the Science teacher was *observed* getting into a car with an unknown and much older man outside Zeon nightclub on Friday night. My scout *observed* she was wobbling more than Amy Winehouse after a let-yourself-go party round Pete Doherty's.

I'm not being bitchy there, am I? If I were bitchy I might

point out to Ms Cooper that white stilettos are downmarket enough even *before* they get sick on them. But I won't. Though I will say that next time you see her you might want to *observe* the right side of her neck. Under the foundation lies a suck-shaped mark. It wouldn't take the CSI team to work out how *that* got there.

I've had a few emails from readers who want to know more about me. I am flattered, of course, and quite frankly need the attention, but I am supposed to be *anonymous*. I realize it's only a matter of time before you figure it out but for now, no deal, as Noel Edmonds said to the six-foot trannie hooker. All I can say is: think of a young Kelly Brook but with a bigger IQ, a smaller nose and less boobage. Hey, we both have brown hair OK? Joking aside, I do like to throw a few crumbs your way from time to time to keep it interesting, so here goes.

I'm a girl and I go to the Adam Woodyatt Academy. There you are. Happy now?

Speaking of crumbs, I'm still on these gluten-free biscuits ever since Mum decided I was allergic just because I said I had a tummy ache after we had pasta on Tuesday. I'd only said I had a tummy ache so I could get out of watching *The Crying Game* with her and Marley as I knew there was a scene coming up (you know the one) which I didn't want to have to explain to either of them. Though I'm sure Mum would have gone off on one about how supportive she'd be if I ever decided to have a gender realignment. No one's realigning my bits, I can tell you.

God, I miss gluten.

Anyways, to judge by the size of my inbox I seem to be attending some kind of special school for social retards. Screw-up Academy, I'm going to start calling you.

Dear Miss Understanding

My boyfriend is nearly perfect, he's buff and says I am too, he writes me little notes saying how much he loves me and when my friend Kayleigh tried to snog him at the ten-pin bowling centre he pushed her away and said, 'I'm spoken for, innit?' Now I know Kayleigh's not that fit, but that counts for something doesn't it?

Anyway, the problem is that he's got bad spots. Some div told him you shouldn't squeeze them cos that makes them worse, but to be honest with you they totally couldn't be any worse. They're huge and yellow and last night one of them popped against my cheek while we were snogging. I had to go and be sick, and when he asked me why I said I'd had too many Bacardi Breezers even though I'd only had three and now he thinks I 'have a problem with alcohol'. He won't buy me anything except J2O since then.

How can I get him to squeeze?

Love

Glorygirl89

Dear Glory

It popped against your face? That's quite a visual. Now it's in my head and won't leave, so thanks for that.

Yeah, Pizza-face sounds irresistible, but perhaps he's not quite as perfect as you think he is. For a start if it's the Kayleigh I'm thinking of, then it really isn't surprising he pushed her away. This is the same Kayleigh who Fat Gareth *literally* ran away from at the school musical after-show party last year. And Fat Gareth A) can't afford to be choosy and B) doesn't run for kicks.

Secondly, he sounds like he's got his priorities all wrong. He's what – sixteen? seventeen? He's more interested in avoiding future facial deformity than making out with a buff sixteen-year-old? I just don't get it. Either he's not really that into you. Or he's so in love with himself he's unaware his skin makes you puke.

But, assuming you genuinely do want to continue seeing this pus-faced control freak, then the solution is simple. Tell him his manly, bristling chin brings you out in a rash and ask him to shave just before he snogs you. No boy possesses enough razor-wielding skill to avoid slicing the tops off his facial volcanoes.

Just make sure you have a tissue handy as you pucker up, sweetheart. Those babies are gonna bleed.

Yours

Miss Understanding

Dear Miss Understanding

My parents hate my boyfriend because they found out he has been in prison. They liked him before so I can't really understand it. I really like him and think he's turned a corner, he's only missed one probation appointment in six months.

How can I make them come round to him?

Yours

Sally

Dear Sally

OK, whoa there, mustang, slow down a little. First you have to convince me that you should keep seeing this guy. I mean, what was he in for? Glamorous diamond thief? Then stick with him. Even if he ends up back inside, he'll probably tell you where he stashed the ice if you occasionally squash a naked boob against the glass during visiting hours.

Two-bit con-man selling double-glazing to grannies? Then probably not. He has no future, unless he gets discovered on that show where they secretly film dodgy tradesmen and he ends up with his own talk show.

Creepy sex-register type? Then definitely not.

Anyway, see where I'm going? I need more info. But if pressed, I'm with your parents on this, dump the jailbird and get yourself a nice lad, like Bradley from *EastEnders*, only not a ginger.

Luvs

Miss U

Dear Miss U

My girlfriend is well fit, but she makes these horrible sucky, gloopy noises when she kisses me. I tried to talk to her about it, but she got offended and told me she was just being passionate. What should I do?

Yours

Turned-off Tariq

Dear Tariq

Been there, done that, got the lip balm. What is it with the sucky people? Can they not hear themselves? It's bad enough we have to watch other couples snogging on buses or in car parks, why do we have to *listen* to them as well? It's not the radio for Christ's sake. We have visual contact.

Would she object if you were to continue listening to your iPod during the snog? Other than that, I can see no easy way out of this one. If you really like her, then tell her straight you can't stand the noise. It'll probably mean the end of the relationship but maybe she'll learn for next time, and you can feel good about having helped her at least part of the way on her turbulent journey through this crazy world.

If you're not that keen then just dump her without saying why and let her next boyfriend deal with it.

Shrugs

Miss Understanding

Well that's all for now. As you know, I'm on the run from the cops, so time for me to snap shut the laptop and head to my next secret hide-out. Hope to have another Miss Understanding Blog for you in a few days.

L8rs losers

Miss U

Miss Understanding Blog Entry
– 11th October 2009

I'll be honest with you, I'm feeling a little unappreciated at the moment. Not only has it come to my attention that certain members of the school teaching fraternity, not happy with chucking me off the school website, have been making efforts to discover my identity with a view to hauling me up in front of Big Head, but also I've had a number of critical responses from members of the student body. *My own people.*

To the person who wrote: 'You suck the bigg one, I bet you is a total minga,' well thanks for your constructive criticism. I shall endeavour to suck smaller ones from now on and pay more attention to my appearance. And to the 'student' who emailed to tell me I was an 'ambassador for my school' and therefore should stop describing the breakfast stains on Mr Williams's tie, I say that it could be so much worse. Of all the stains I could be pointing out, what's a little dried egg yolk between teachers and pupils?

So lighten up people!

It wasn't all bad. Jenna Hall emailed to say, 'Thanks for the laughs; you make me see how funny school can be.' Which was nice. 'You're tops, Miss Understanding,' writes Charlie Chambers, 'fancy a shag?' Er, well, if you're the Charlie who has a fringe that makes him look like the Dulux dog, then I'm all right, thanks.

Today I'm listening to Linkin Park because Jake lent me all three CDs. It's just some incredibly loud, distorted guitars with the mixing volume turned down just enough so you can hear some bloke shouting incomprehensibly into a mic over the top. Hellooo? Mr Park? Why not just play the guitars quieter in the first place? Then you wouldn't have to shout and we could hear what you are so angry about.

Still, what do I know about music? Films, now I know something about films. Mum got it totally wrong at the DVD shop last night and came back with *Angus, Thongs and Perfect Snogging*. Now I used to love the Louise Rennison books but I'm getting a bit old for them now. And as for poor old Marley, well he hardly got through the credits before he had to go and be sick. 'Why are they giggling the whole time?' he asked. 'What's so funny about kissing?' I'm with you there, Marley bruv. I quite liked it secretly, even if it was a little young for me. I wonder if the author is going to let the main character (Georgia) grow up and start moving beyond the snogging stage? I bet she'd like to, but isn't allowed. After all, they toned down the title for the film, it was *Angus, Thongs and Full-Frontal Snogging* for the book. That's Hollywood for you. I wonder what the other cleaned-up film titles would be? *Stop in the Name of Undergarments* or *Knocked out by my Winning Smile* perhaps? Let's Blue-sky it. Email me your ideas for toned-down Louise Rennison titles and I'll post the best suggestions.

Moving right on, I was talking to my BFF Crumpet the other day (and remember Reader, all names are changed to protect the innocent) and she told me she saw The Boy eating the face of some girl from the estate in Clifton. For those of you new to the blog and ignorant of local geography, Clifton is a little village on the Oxfordshire border up the hill. I used to happily live there before my folks split like an infinitive (that's a very clever literary joke, you know . . . oh never mind).

(Also, someone asked me to explain who all these people are I keep talking about. Briefly – Poop-chute is going out with Jugs. Crumpet has been my best friend for ages. Jake just kind of floats about and The Boy is . . . well, he's this boy I've liked for years and we've had this sort of on-again off-again thing. Every time I think it's going somewhere he screws up. Half the time he's planning our future together and telling me he's going to keep out of trouble and then next thing I know he's left me sitting alone in some dodgy café wondering how long I should give him *this* time.)

Anyway turns out on this occasion he also had his hand down this girl's top. Now this is about a six out of ten on the downer scale. Not because he has chosen another girl but because it proves yet again that my judgement is well dodgy when it comes to members of the opposite sex. God alone knows why anyone would take advice from me. Yes, me, the biggest disaster the dating world has ever seen. The thing is, I just know what kind of boy my mum would like me to go out with. A creative, middle-class type from the posh side of town. And I'm going out of my way to fancy the opposite. An illiterate loser from the *Crimewatch* side of town. Yeah, bring it on. If only to see the look of disappointment on Mum's face.

Anyway, enough about sad old me, must get on to fixing other people's problems.

Dear Miss Understanding

My girlfriend, let's call her Nelly, broke up with me just before Christmas and I cried so hard it made my nose bleed. I gave all my Christmas presents to charity I was so miserable.

13

Anyway, I thought I'd got over her and started going out with another girl. But last week I saw Nelly at the skating park snogging Guy DuLancey and I fell to bits again.

My new girlfriend wants to know what's wrong, but I can't tell her. I like the new one, but still love Nelly.

Please, please help!

Loverboy92

Dear Loverboy

Oh Lordy, sounds like you've got more unwanted baggage than Heathrow's lost property department. Few things:

1) Why is giving your Chrimbo pressies to charity going to make you feel better? That's the dumbest thing I ever heard.

2) I assume your ex-girlfriend's real name is Kelly. No one's called Nelly, except Nelly Furtado . . . or Nelly the Elephant. (Note to wannabe spies: when disguising names, make sure you don't just change the first letter.) Furthermore, it's pretty clear you're talking about Kelly Binns, aka Super-slag. She's the only Kelly that hangs around the skate park (my spies reveal).

3) I feel justified in revealing her identity because she called me a flat-chested bee-yatch *on my first day*!

4) Also I'm not too pleased with your behaviour either, you know? Who died and made you the new Russell

Brand? Do you really think I'm going to be sympathetic to some love-sick puppy who goes out with the 'new one' just to try and help him get over his slag-lust? If you hold baggage, it's your duty to drop it off before you get on board the next plane.

Solution: break up (gently) with 'the New One', then fart in a bottle and take a whiff every time you think about Super-slag. Oh, and in helping to get over her, you might want to aware yourself of the fact she once gave Sean O'Doherty a hand job during assembly.

Byeee

Miss Trying-really-hard-to-be Understanding

Dear Miss Understanding

I hate my mum's new boyfriend. He is such a knob. And don't say it's because I miss my dad because I like soooo don't. How can I get him to leave her?

Yours

Grumpy

Dear Hamlet

You're being vague; you know I don't like that. How can I help you people if you don't give me the material? It's like going to the doctor and saying, 'I am unwell,' and when he says, 'What are your symptoms?' you just say, 'Bits of my body feel bad.' I'm not House MD, OK?!

15

Still, having got that off my not-at-all-flat chest, getting rid of new 'uncles' is easy. There are two approaches. Firstly you could start calling him Dad, or better yet, Daddy. That'll creep him out, especially if you start hugging him and crying a bit when he's trying to watch the football.

If that doesn't work, then tell your mother he keeps 'accidentally' popping into the bathroom when you're having a shower.

If he's still there in a month, then stage a play in the living room, lose a duel and poison everyone.

Sorted,

Miss Understanding

Laters lemmings.

PS Someone who was in a staff room and saw a memo they shouldn't have tells me that Mr Collins thinks he knows who I am and is going to 'flush me out' like I'm some kind of foreign object lodged in an ear canal.

Well, come on then Syringe-man, do your worst.

Miss I-will-not-be-moved, Understand?

Miss Understanding Blog Entry
– 19th October 2009

I was talking to my friend Crumpet the other day about the environment. We've been doing this project about waste and recycling and stuff. 'I never understood the problem with landfill sites,' Crumpet says to me. 'If we don't fill land, then we'll just end up with big holes everywhere.'

And can I just say, Crumpet got eleven GCSES and came second in her year. If she's the cream of the new generation, this planet is doomed. Sorry. We may as well all buy the new, six-litre fuel-injected Ford Clarkson on a credit card, swathe the planet in plastic bags and make our last few years as comfortable as possible.

On to Boy News:

Hmmm, now not sure what to make of this. So thought I'd just cut-n-paste and ask for *your* advice this time. Received this yesterday.

Dear Miss Understanding

I am a guy, sixteen, at your school. I think I know who you are, and if you are who I think you are, I just wanted to let you know I fancy you. I can't work up the courage to say it to your face, but I think you're really pretty and sweet.

Only thing is, I've started reading your blogs, and I don't really think I like them. Now don't get me wrong, I think you're funny and clever, where did you learn to write like that? Not at Woodyatt I reckon. But I think sometimes people really need help and you don't give them the right advice.

Sorry to come at you out of the blue like this, but hope you understand. I'd feel bad if I didn't say what I thought.

Yours

Average-looking-but-quite-sweet-if-slightly-bumbling-guy

OK, so my first thought was that this is a teacher pretending to be a boy at my school in the hope of flushing me out. Like a reverse honey-trap. But then I thought, what if it's genuine? What if there is some well-fit boy with a secret crush on me (or on some better-looking girl he thinks is me, more likely), what would I do? Since people have been calling me insensitive recently, let's take this at face value and see where it gets us.

So, Average-looking-but-quite-sweet-if-slightly-bumbling-guy (can I call you Al?). I want you on the table, er . . . but not in a weird way. I think you should make yourself known to me. Let's talk about this over a smoothie at The Bridge Café – if you're easy on the eye, I might let you live. You know where to find me, just tell me when in a private SMS. Or send another email to Anya@missunderstanding.net. Just be prepared for me to publish and be damned.

Gossip Corner. In keeping with the current theme of secret identities, I won't directly name today's featured teachers. So who were the two mystery staff members seen furtively exiting the sick room on Tuesday, looking anything but sick, and ever so slightly dishevelled? Answers by email please.

OK, emails. I love 'em, Keep sending them, by all that's short and curly, I do love to read about your tragic lives.

Dear Miss Understanding
I'm sixteen, straight and female.

I've been seeing this guy; I'll call him Trev, which is nothing like his real name, before you start trying to guess. He's really sweet and I like him a lot. He's not pushing me or anything, but I think I want to sleep with him. I hadn't planned to have sex until I was eighteen. But I feel I'm ready now. His parents are away this weekend and he's invited me over. Mum thinks

I'm staying at my friend's house so we've got all night.

I've already been out and got condoms. Should I go through with it?

Kisses

Worried

Dear Worried

I can't make that decision for you, but let's face it; you're going to do it anyway, aren't you? You just want me to give you my approval.

I'm not going to do that. That's got to be your choice and if you're unsure, then *definitely* don't do it. And if you do go ahead with it, be careful, OK? Don't forget the condoms, don't forget to put one on, and don't forget to tie a knot in it afterwards or else you'll be scrubbing the carpet at two in the morning.

Let me know how it came out, as it were.

Love

Miss U

Via text:

DEAR MISSES UNDERSTANDING,

ALL RIGHT?

HOW CAN I GET THIS GIRL TO GO OUT WIV ME, BRUV? I TXTD HER AND AKSED HER TO GO TO THE CLUB AT THE UNI ON SAT

COS YOU KNOW THEY DON'T CHECK YOUR ID BUTT SHE SAID SHE WAS WASHING HER HAIR. THEN MY MATE BEK SEZ SHE'S ONLY OUT AT ZEON ON SAT WIV HER M8S. WOT SHOULD I DO? SHE'S BARE FIT AND I RECKON SHE'D PUT OUT AFTER A BIT OF CIDER.

GEX

Dear Gex

You sound quite a catch. Sure this girl's right for you? Why don't you forget about her and ride off with me on the back of your skateboard?

No? Oh well. What I suggest, Gex, apart from learning some remedial English, is that you put your actual face in front of her actual face and actually 'aks' her, IRL and F2F, if she'd like to go to the club with you. Hmmm?

Eye contact is the key here. Leave your mobile at home and talk to the girl.

Oh and one more thing. Smile. Girls like that.

Good luck

Miss I-give-up-on-these-people Understanding

Blue Sky Corner – OK, I asked you to come up with suggestions for more wholesome titles for the film versions of Louise Rennison books. I was deluged by an avalanche. I weeded out the libellous and the pornographic (I said tone down, you morons) and here are the best of the rest.

Luuurve is a Many-Trousered Thing should really be, *Luuurve is a Silver-Ring Thing*, says the canny Georgia Banks.

It's OK, I'm wearing Really Big Knickers could become *It's OK, I'm wearing Thick Woollen Tights* suggests Sonia Bailey.

Blake Grimshaw thinks *Dancing in my Nuddy-Pants* might be more accessible if it were changed to *Dancing in my Sensible Shoes*.

And That's When It Fell Off In My Hand reads much better as *And That's When It All Went Amiss* according to Jared Freeman.

Bubbles Gosling seems to think '. . . *Then He Ate my Boy Entrancers* should really be changed to *Then he Ate my Pumpkin Pie*, but quite frankly I think that's ruder.

And finally, Ben Noakes says '. . . *Startled by His Furry Shorts* could be *Startled by His Furry Hamster*. Same comment, Ben.

Miss Understanding Blog Entry
– 10th November 2009

Bonjour M. Woodyatt. Today we parlez in la Franglais, d'accord? After tout, our French oral examinacion is très prochaine. *Nous* must practise! Maintenant! Nouveau this semaine, je . . .

Oh mon dieu, I can't keep it up.

Had a bit of a *conversation* with Mum earlier tonight. I mention it because we don't have a lot of conversations in our house. This is on account of Jocasta (as I'm going to call her) not being at home very much:

'What *are* you wearing?' I said, as she moved around the teetering kitchen trying to find things under piles.

'What? This? It's a smock,' my mother said. Her flyaway blonde hair floated winsomely about her as she passed the open window.

'You look like Miffy,' I pointed out. 'Please tell me you're not starting ceramics again.'

'I'm not starting ceramics *again*,' she said. 'I never gave up on the ceramics. I have been resting. Besides, I can't find the clay.'

'Oh, I chucked it,' I said.

'What? Why, darling?'

'Because Marley was eating it.' Which was true. Marley *had* been eating it. He eats everything. Took me ages to work out why I was getting through so much Daniel Frieda Brilliant Brunette.

'Oh,' Jocasta said, not at all concerned. 'Funny little fellow.'

'So, if you're not doing pottery,' I went on. 'Why are you dressed like an apple farmer?'

'I told you, darling,' she said airily whilst rummaging through a drawer, 'I'm off on my retreat this weekend. I just need to find my keys.'

'This very weekend? You're leaving . . . now?' I closed my eyes and thumped my head down on to the French book resting open on the wooden table in front of me.

'Yes, I'm sure I mentioned it this morning.'

'No, you said you were going to work on your aura this weekend and that you'd rather I didn't play the new White Stripes album any more.'

'He has a terribly jarring voice,' Jocasta said, trying to gather up all of her unruly hair in order to shove it through a scrunchie. 'And Meg's drumming isn't all it could—'

24

'Look, sorry to interrupt you, Simon Cowell,' I said, 'but just to be absolutely clear – does this mean I'm babysitting again?'

'Oh sweetheart. Marley doesn't need babysitting. He's seven.'

'He's *six*!!' I cried, losing it finally. 'And the only reason you think he doesn't need babysitting is because you don't ever do it. You always get me to look after him. When's the last time you made him dinner?'

'He cooks for himself, like you, clever boy. Marley is extremely independent. He made himself a toasted sandwich the other day.'

'Yes, with birthday cake and ketchup filling.'

Mum stopped her faffing and sat down opposite me. She tried to give me her I-love-you-really-you-know look.

'Sweetheart, you know it's been difficult for me since your father and I split.'

'What are you talking about?' I said, rolling my eyes. 'It hasn't been difficult for *you* at all. Dad bought you this house; he sends you money so you don't need to work. You spend most evenings out with your friends or off doing your yoga, or Reiki or Scientology. The only course you haven't done is the Staying at Home and Cooking Your Kids a Decent Bloody Meal one.'

'Darling, I do appreciate you, you know. Both of you,'

she said, fingertips to her lined forehead. 'You're such wonderful people; if you weren't so strong I . . . I don't know what I'd do.'

At this point I simply gaped at the woman who gave birth to me. People? I thought. We're not people. I'm a teenager and Marley's a child. Why does she treat us like we're her support group?

'Don't give me that, Mum,' I said. 'Last week you packed us off to Devon with Gran and Grandpa so you could have some rest. Because we're just so exhausting, aren't we? And now we're back, you're off on a retreat for the whole weekend. Retreating from *what* I'd like to know. Is it us?'

She stared back at me for ages, then, 'It's not you,' she half whispered in a cracked voice. 'My migraine's coming back.' She massaged her temples. 'I'll be back Sunday night darling. You can call your father if you need anything; he's only a fifteen-minute drive away. Please don't forget to put the bins out.'

I listened to the front door slam and sat staring at the wall for a bit. Then I popped upstairs to check on Marley. He was sleeping face down, still wearing his Wolverine outfit. Poor Marley. He'd spent most of the day lying on top of the bookshelf in the hall waiting for one of us to walk by so he could slice the top of our heads off. As Jocasta had been downstairs engrossed in Tom Cruise's biography and I'd been lying on my bed, moaning and listening to the *Juno* soundtrack, he'd had a disappointing haul of scalps.

I removed his claws and left him to it. Then I went back downstairs, opened a tin of beans and tipped them into a saucepan on the Aga. I sat back at the table, gave up the French for the night and decided to write a little bit to people who might care about my tragic life.

What would I do without you, my friends?

PS OK, in a BBC News-style effort to produce balanced reporting I should point out my discovery of a Sainsbury's New York cheesecake and a Waitrose banoffee pie in our fridge, for me and Marley respectively. I should also point out that Waitrose and Sainsbury's are not exactly close to one another. My mother schlepped all the way from one side of Allerton to the other to get each of us the treats we like. It nearly kills me to admit it, but Jocasta is actually quite a kind person when she tries.

PPS This doesn't make up for the rest of it.

PPPS This cheesecake is bloody lovely, though.

Yes, almost all of you got it right. The two teachers popping out of the gym store cupboard last week were none other than Mr Graves the PE teacher, and Ms Cooper, the flame-haired vixen of Adam Woodyatt Academy. Not content with digging for gold at Zeon, she's taking time out of her busy schedule to help deflate Mr Graves' balls.

I meant *basket* balls!

Hi there Anya, it is Anya, isn't it? I mean, you are Anya? And also Miss Understanding? Anyway, enough of this smooth talk. I'd really like to meet up with you. The Bridge Café sounds great, how about 5.30 on Thursday? PM I mean. After school.

Yours

Al

Miss Understanding Blog Entry
– 2nd December 2009

First things first. I need to quickly fix your lives for you before I depress you with tragic tales of my own dismal existence.

Dear Miss Understanding

I'm male, straight and sixteen.

Help me! I'm in love. Problem is, it's with a teacher. I can't say who, but she's beautiful, and only a few years older than me. Madonna was like ten years older than Guy Ritchie. So it's not *that* weird is it?

Anyway, I think she likes me too; she's always laughing at my jokes and gives me much better marks than I get from any of the other teachers – and Bonny Greaves said she saw her checking out my butt in Assembly. I can't concentrate on my History essay because I'm always thinking about her.

Should I ask her out?

Jube93

Dear Jube

Jube? . . . Jube? . . . Hello? Anyone home?

Let's pretend for an instant, that your brain is not totally overwhelmed by testosterone and that this woman does have a stupid crush on you. For the love of Davina McCall, can't you see this is only going to end in bad times?

Chances are if you stripped naked and offered yourself to her on a plate she'd slap your spotty backside and send you back home to mummy, but on the million-to-one chance that she'd lose control of her sanity and enter into a summer-spring romance with you, it would only be a matter of time before you both get found out. She'd get fired, you'd be grounded for the rest of your days and do nothing but cry into your pillow and spout awful poetry when you should be studying for your History finals.

You don't love her. Leave her alone. Find a girl your own age. Or better yet, leave all the girls alone until you've finished school. That's what uni's for.

Yours

Miss Cruel-to-be-Kind Understanding

Dear Miss U

Mum won't let me go to Kelly Binns's party on Saturday. Any advice on how I could make her change her mind?

    Yours

    Bluegrass

Dear Bluegrass

What!?? Super-slag Binns is having a party and this is how I find out about it?! I feel snubbed. The social event of the season so far and my invitation seems to have gone astray. I'm truly gutted, everyone knows Mr Binns works for Yoof Beverages and the rumour is he's bringing in two tankers-full of alcopop, one blue and the other red. Which I guess means the flowerbeds on the Brickford estate are going to be a lovely shade of purple come Saturday morning.

Seriously though, are you sure you want to go to this party? I can tell you now how it's all going to pan out:

7.30 pm – losers arrive, sober and dull

8.30 pm – everyone else arrives, pre-loaded and menacing

9.30 pm – discussion and sampling of ringtones

10.30 pm – discussion and sampling of nose-rings

11.00 pm – losers' curfew

11.30 pm – first vomit.

12.30 am – first fight

1.00 am – first vomit during fight

1.30 am – people start refusing to go home when asked

2.30 am – shoving match on pavement with complaining neighbours

3.30 am – Team Asbo arrive with drugs

4.30 am – police arrive.

Then next morning everyone will check Facebook to find out what they got up to and they'll be talking for weeks about just how many litres of alcopop were pumped out of Saskia Garfield's stomach, or how many stitches Jez Morton got above his left eye and how many boys had their hands down Kelly Binns's jeans during the course of the party . . .

Actually, come to mention it, it does sound like fun. Maybe I should chavcrash? No one knows me anyway, they'll just think I'm some local hooch.

Look, getting permission to go is easy, tell your mum it's not actually a party but a charity event organized by Kelly's parents to raise money for a life-saving operation in America. If she asks for details tell her Kelly needs an urgent personality transplant as hers is twisted and decaying.

See you there!

Miss Understanding

That's all for now on the email front. The rest of you were either too dull to bother with, or too tragic to cope with. *You* decide. Now, on to my own issues, and don't think you can slope off, you only have to read this stuff, I have to live it.

Hi there Miss Understanding

I've developed a crush on a funny girl who writes an agony column on her blog page. I had a coffee with her the other day and I think it went quite well, though she was a bit reserved. Also, she laughed a little *too* loudly when I spilt mocha in my crotch. But nonetheless, I think she's really sweet and funny and I'd like to ask her to go out on a proper date with me, do you think that's a good idea? And if so, where should I take her? What should I wear? How should I behave?

    Yours

    Average-looking-but-quite-sweet-if-slightly-bumbling-guy

Dear Al

This girl sounds *amazing*. Are you sure you're in her ball park? I get the impression she likes dashing rogues who buy expensive presents.

I'd say go for it, but you'd really have to be on your game. Suggest to meet under the clock on the high street.

I'd recommend pink roses (but have these delivered to her house earlier on the day because she doesn't want to be lugging the sodding things around all night) and a trip to the cinema to watch a romantic comedy that you should let her choose. You should definitely offer to pay. She may order the large popcorn, don't be put off by this, or take it as an invitation to share. You should get your own, you cheap loser.

After the cinema, walk her home and don't try to kiss her unless she's making it clear she wants you to.

Hope this helps?

Yours

Miss-Hoping-I-haven't-Misunderstood

Email to Crumpet@notmail.com

Hey Crumps,

Have I told you I hate school? OK, maybe not hate, just dislike intensely. I don't know anyone here, and they all know each other from Year Seven or because their parents are friends. There are only a dozen or so students here from outside the area which is basically because the school's a bit rubbish really. Mum thinks it'll be good for me, that Clifton was too middle-class. As if *she* isn't. If you looked up middle-class in the dictionary, there'd be a picture of my mother drinking a glass of Chablis.

I just keep myself to myself really and everyone

ignores me. I know I'm mouthy with you guys, but for some reason here I can just never think of anything to say. I go home straight after school, usually because I have to cook Marley's dinner and then do my homework and then clean the house because Mum's in bed with her migraines again.

I miss you all so much. Anyway, let me tell you about the school. It's much bigger than Clifton, and it's an academy, which is supposed to mean they're allowed to raise funds from a range of local sources, 'thereby forging links with the business and charitable sectors'. What it means, really, is that they trouser 100K from BigBurger every year in exchange for some minor alterations to the curriculum.

Not saying the school's being commercialized or anything but last week in History we were asked to come up with new meal-combos for Henry VIII and each of his wives. Henry had a swan-burger, large fries and a giant shake, Anne of Cleves had the salad 'cos she's so boring, Anne Boleyn had a burger with the top cut off. There was the Catherine of Tarragon chicken wrap, and the Catherine Parr-ty bucket of ribs, and so on – to be honest, it was a laugh.

It's a bit rough though – last term there were two stabbings, three pregnancies and a heroin overdose. And that's just the teachers. Maybe it'll get better. Maybe I'll make some friends in the New Year. Stranger things have happened. Like this very weekend when Marley got tangled in the Klunt shelving system in the showroom bit of IKEA and they had to free him with bolt-cutters.

Email soon, yeah, let me know what you're all up to? How's Jugs? Seen much of The Boy? Did he mention me?

Love

An

Miss Understanding Blog Entry
– 12th December 2009

Saturday night was Binns night. I dragged poor Al along even though he's not been keen on Kelly since she punched him during a game of football when they were in junior school and knocked out a tooth.

My goodness, didn't we have fun! If you were there, you probably didn't notice me. I dressed to fit in and had my hoodie up all night. My favourite bit was when Guy DuLancey fell out of the first-floor window, landed on the conservatory roof and just lay there while everyone danced under him, looking like the world's worst glitter-ball.

I wasn't so keen on the drinking games in the kitchen, or the film some boys were watching in the sitting room that had lots of ladies not wearing very much. But the music was pretty good and I even persuaded Al to dance with me. The house looked totally trashed by the time we left, just before 11.00. Imogen Chivers emailed to say she asked Kelly what she was going to tell her parents about the mess and Kelly looked about and said, 'What? It always looks like this.'

I heard that Kelly ended up letting at least five boys have a go on her boobs. At least she finished the night with the boy who'd started the evening as her boyfriend. So that's nice.

On Sunday my brother Marley (aka Wolverine) and I were invited to my father's house for a Christmas BBQ. What's that? I hear you say. A Christmas BBQ? Who has a BBQ at Christmas? What are you talking about? Have you gone insane, Miss Understanding?

I'll tell you who has a Christmas BBQ. People with a giant marquee and half a dozen patio heaters, that's who. I realize you need a bit of background, so here goes:

The invitation came from my father's new wife. My long-term readers will know that this woman is named Cheryl and that I've only met her once before, on their wedding day, when she wasn't really with it.

So basically I've never properly met the woman who my dad intends to spend the rest of his life with. Cheryl and Dad moved into their new house (which Dad designed and which has won an architecture award – all glass and steel and concrete and half of it underground) last year and before I'd had a chance to pop around for a visit, Mum moved me and Wolverine here, thirty miles away, to the other side of the Chilterns and to a totally new school. Mum refuses to even acknowledge Cheryl's existence. When she has to refer to the woman who lives in Dad's house, she just calls her the Housekeeper.

So, back to the BBQ. Marley and I rock up in a taxi; Mum refuses to go anywhere near the place. She says it looks like the Teletubbies' house and that she's worried she might get sucked up by the Noo-noo. She's jealous; our house in Allerton is a crumbly Victorian semi with bits stuck on the front and back. Dad's house is a futuristic vision set into a steep hillside with a spectacular view. The kind of place a Bond villain might build to intimidate his enemies and get off with women in. Marley loved it, particularly when he discovered the loo had a floor-to-ceiling window so you can see Oxford's dreaming spires twenty miles away while you're doing a poo. Only laser cannon in the roof would have topped that for my little brother.

Cheryl had told us to dress up, so Wolverine had his best claws on and I'd thrown all caution to the wind down at Top Shop and bought some bright red leggings. I wore my shortest denim skirt, a very wide belt and my bestest Primani bag.

Cheryl came out to meet us as we crunched up the gravel path, our breath misting. She was wearing this amazing bright red dress and was tiny-stick-thin, like Keira Knightley with a tapeworm.

'Darling!' she said, giving me a slow air-kiss on both cheeks. She turned to Marley and raised a thin eyebrow. He looked terrified but took off a claw and shook her hand bravely. I couldn't get over how amazing she looked.

'I'm so glad you're here,' Cheryl said, beaming at me and totally defying that old image of a wicked stepmother. She took us through the house, showing it off, real pride in her voice. She wasn't just boasting at how big and expensive it was, she really loved it. And I realized she'd put a lot of herself into it too. Dad designed the outside. The hard, cold bits. Cheryl had added the 'female touch'. She'd softened the hard edges with drapes and rugs, she'd brought colour in with cushions and wall-hangings. It looked like something out of a catalogue. I could see why Mum didn't like coming here; she'd stand out like Paris Hilton at a pub quiz.

'Your father had to pop down to the station to pick someone up,' Cheryl said. And then with a wink, added, 'Gives us girls a chance to bond.' She'd obviously already forgotten about Marley, not that he cared.

The BBQ was well underway in the back garden. Cheryl nabbed a couple of glasses of bubbly from a waitress. Who has catering at a BBQ? The last BBQ we had at Mum's wasn't so well-organized. Mum set fire to the rabbit hutch and Marley had the runs for a week.

The marquee was more of a canopy, covering the space between the back of the house and a stylish, low-maintenance walled garden. I liked all that but wasn't so sure about the half-dozen or so tall granite-effect sculptures dotted around like a stone circle bought from Argos. To be honest, they looked a bit like giant willies. Maybe they were supposed to be some kind of fertility symbol. Hope Cheryl isn't of a mind to provide me with a step-sibling. According to most fairy-tales they're nothing but trouble for all concerned and, after helping to raise a little Marley, I for one don't want to have to change a nappy again until I've at least doubled my age.

There were maybe thirty people there, mostly Cheryl's age, late-thirties, early-forties. These were her friends rather than my dad's. My brother was obsessed with the koi carp, fat splashes of gold and red, twisting and flipping their tails out of the water occasionally. He sat on a stone plinth and watched them like a cat while Cheryl introduced me about. 'This is Portia, she's in publishing. Here's Venetia, she's in litigation, etc.'

'This is Jeremy,' she said, drawing me up to a young man wearing a grey suit with no tie. 'He's doing an installation in Hoxton.'

'Satellite dish?' I asked.

'No, darling, Jeremy is a *conceptual artist*. I mean he's doing an *artistic* installation.'

'Oh, brilliant,' I said, turning the same colour as my leggings. Jeremy told me he was circumventing traditional notions of illumination in art by creating a light-free space in a physical mindscape.

I had to think about this. 'You turn the lights off?'

He shook his head. I obviously hadn't understood. 'I de-install the source of illumination. The art must be viewed by the untempered mind, free from visual stimulation.'

I nodded, slowly backing away.

'And this is Seth,' Cheryl said spinning me around to see the most beautiful boy there has ever been and ever will be. He looked like he'd been designed by a team of German scientists with maybe an Italian on board as a style consultant. He was tanned and had dark hair in a fashionable cut but without going overboard. He smiled at me and I nearly toppled into the agapanthus. 'His mother is Portia Bolt-Hodges, she knows your mother,' Cheryl whispered. 'He's just joined a broker's firm in the City.'

'Hi,' he said.

'Mmmpffchun,' I replied, trying to put my tongue back in. I had met Seth before, I remembered – about ten years ago – and he hadn't looked like that!

'Seth has just come back from his gap year in Africa,' Cheryl said. 'He was helping to run an orphanage in Mali.'

'Well,' Seth said, tilting his head modestly. 'I don't know about helping to run. I played football with the kids and filled in a few forms.'

'And raised thirty thousand pounds,' Cheryl said.

'Wow!' was my lame contribution as I stared at Golden Boy.

He glanced at Cheryl, and then back at me, perhaps wondering if I was a bit backward. I realized I had to say something . . . anything.

'So, Africa hey? What . . . what . . . what's that like?'

He closed his eyes and I watched him smile as he remembered. 'Amazing, beyond words. There's music everywhere, the people are friendly and funny and interesting. There's so much life there, so much colour.' As he spoke he opened his eyes again and looked around at the gloomy, grey day and the style-conscious people floating around dispiritedly.

'I do hope we're not too much of a disappointment to you back here in England,' Cheryl said, laughing.

'Not at all,' he said, and I think for a second he glanced at me.

'Tell me about the animals,' I asked. 'Did you see any lions?'

'Once I saw a lion, yes, on safari. I also saw loads of hippos. Did you know they're much more dangerous than lions?'

'Really? Do they eat you?'

'They'll kill you, though the funny thing is, they're vegetarians. They'd happily bite you in half, but then just spit the bits out.'

'Oh that's all right then,' I said. 'Being bitten in half is bad enough. Spending your last few seconds watching a hippo swallow your legs would be just *too* much.'

It wasn't a great joke, though Seth laughed politely and Cheryl fell about like I was Ricky Gervais or something. If she'd been texting she would have written ROTFLMAO! Seth raised his eyebrows at me and I melted. But then we were interrupted by a kerfuffle behind us.

'Daddy!' someone said and I turned to see my father standing stiffly, looking down at Marley, who was wrapped around his leg. Dad had dyed his hair and may even have been wearing manscara. Either way he appeared to be at least five years younger than the last time I'd seen him. He's like that, my dad. Never quite what you remembered from before. Like the *Time Traveller's Wife*'s Husband. I walked up, feeling shy. He hugged me awkwardly. Cheryl was obviously delighted to see this reunion and skittered around like a daddy-long-legs with ADD.

'Beautiful,' she said. 'Perfect.'

She was right. I haven't had such a nice time since I left Clifton. I miss my old life. And even though Dad has a new wife and a new house and a new haircut, just then I felt more at home than I do down the hill in Allerton. I sipped champagne and went a bit silly. I chatted about modern art and architecture; I giggled with Cheryl, and laughed with Dad. Everything was perfect.

Until Marley screwed it all up, of course.

We all heard a scream and spun to see the little idiot on top of one of the stone willies, scrabbling for grip as the thing wobbled and began to topple. I could hear the men around me wince as they saw his claws dig in. It was like a Ben Stiller film, everything slowing down and people shouting 'Noooooooooooo . . .' as the huge stone member went over. Marley didn't even have the decency to look scared as he went down. Like the rest of us, he could see he was headed straight for one of the black pools. The little monster flicked out three long claws and disappeared into the water with a flump and a sploosh. A gaggle of interior designers standing on the wrong side of the pond were drenched with frog spawn.

When he came up, he was spitting out water and we stared in horror to see a fat koi writhing against his knuckles, a look of astonishment on its dumb fish-face as it flapped, skewered by three eight-inch aluminium claws. My little brother, for his part looked immensely pleased with himself. This had recently, and rather abruptly, stopped being my perfect day, but was still very much his.

I was mortified, and avoided Seth's eye as we dragged

a sodden Marley into the house to get changed.

As we got into the cab to go home, Marley now looking like an understuffed scarecrow in some of Dad's old clothes, Cheryl stopped me.

'Maybe you should come around for dinner, darling,' she said, her eyes flicking over at my brother. 'Just you, you know, for a . . . well, so we can get to know each other properly.'

I nearly burst into tears, dear readers. Cheryl didn't need me. Why should she care about her new husband's children? We'd just messed up her très sophistique garden party; we'd embarrassed her in front of her friends. And yet here she was, reaching out to me and giving me a second chance.

I know you're not supposed to like the woman who replaces your mum. And I know I should have been miffed that Marley wasn't invited, but I so wanted to come to dinner and on my own.

So I said yes.

Oh gotta go, Blogpals. Jocasta's calling me for dinner. Wish me luck.

L8rs.

Email to jugs@notmail.com
Hey Bird,
What you hayseeds doing up on the hill these days.

Making moonshine? Home dentistry? Marrying cousins? Here in the big smoke things're sure different. They have multicoloured lights at intersections to tell you when to stop and when to go. They have intersections. They have moving stairs in the department stores. They have department stores.

Just kidding. I wanted to tell you about this date I had. I'll try and call later. Or you call me? I can't talk to Mum about that sort of thing any more, Marley would just make vomiting noises throughout and though I've met some nice people at school I don't really have anyone that close I can talk to. Worst of all I can't put it up on the blog as Al has asked me if we could keep things off-record. That feels a bit weird. I put *everything* on the blog. I guess I'll do as he asks for now, but if this is going to go anywhere, he's got to get used to the fact that my private life is public. Nor do I intend to self-censor for fear of offending him, he's gotta take me warts and all.

Sheesh, don't I sound the little madam? I just read that back. We've had one sort-of date and I'm laying down rules and telling him how it should be.

Anyways, hope to see ya soon

Luv

Anya

Miss Understanding Blog Entry
– 22nd December 2009

I had a text from The Boy today. Did you know that the heart is just a four-valve pump? All it does is move blood around the body, so that white blood cells can carry oxygen to where it's needed. That's it. That's all the heart is.

So why the hell does it leap about like a deranged flamenco dancer whenever The Boy's name appears on my inch-square phone screen? How exactly does that work, Mr Bellamy the Biology teacher? They're just abbreviated words, from an abbreviated intellect, in a guy, who, let's be entirely frank here, isn't that good-looking anyway. Yes he has that smile, and his eyes have those little crow's feet that make you feel light-headed when he leans towards you so he can hear what you're saying when it's noisy in the pub. But he isn't Jake Gyllenhaal. He isn't Brad Pitt and he isn't that bloke with the stupid-yet-surprisingly-sexy haircut from *High School Musical 3*. He's just The Boy, for God's sake.

And he honestly means nothing to me.

Anyway, what he said in his text was quite interesting. Apparently Jugs and Poop-chute have split up. I knew something like this would happen, as soon as I left. Phoned Jugs but she wouldn't pick up. Need to talk to Jocasta about spending a few days back in Clifton. It might mean she'll have to spend some time alone with Marley, so God knows whether it will happen.

Oh wells, check out the three new agonizing emails below.

Kisses – mwah mwah

Miss Understanding

Dear Miss Understanding

I think my fella is a kleptomaniac. He's always nicking things. Whenever we go shopping I'm just looking around at stuff and he's right beside me then suddenly he's gone and I look up to see him being chased down the street by a security guard.

He pinches stupid stuff he doesn't need, like padlocks and chargers that don't fit his phone and reams of copier paper. But just when I'm thinking of dumping him, he goes and nicks the lipstick I've been saving up for. Plus he's not been caught yet which means he's smart, right?

Yours

Cat

Hey Cat

Hmmm, that's a toughie. Free lipsticks are a powerful draw. It reminds me of the joke about the family who take their son to the doctor because he thinks he's a chicken. 'Have you tried hypnotherapy?' the doctor asks them. 'Oh we don't want to cure him,' they say. 'We need the eggs.'

OK, how about this? Tell him you want him to nick something well expensive, like a diamond ring. If he gets caught, he'll go to jail, in which case the problem's taken out of your hands. Or if he gets away with it, then you get yourself a lovely ring.*

Yours

Miss light-fingered Understanding

*Please note this advice is not intended to be taken seriously. The owners of Missunderstanding.net do not accept any responsibility whatsoever for any criminal records or loss of earnings suffered as a result of some idiot taking me at face value.

Dear Miss Understanding,

You know how when you ask your friend if your bum looks big in something and she pauses a bit too long before saying no? Well that's happened to me a few times and now after extensive research with two mirrors in my mum's bathroom I realize I have a massive butt. I've been doing loads of exercise and I'm thin everywhere else but the bum blubber won't shift and being thin above and below just makes it look worse in comparison, I look like an anaconda that's swallowed a Space Hopper.

My boyfriend wants me to go to Malaga with him and his family in August and I'm dreading having to wear a bikini, any advice?

Kate

Hi Kate

Not Kate Nash by any chance, are you? She's obsessed with bums too.

Look don't worry about it. No one really cares, no one's really looking, and even if they are, lots of blokes like big bums anyway. Don't you think there's something a little worrying about boys who like girls who have bottoms like other boys? Erm, not that I'm saying there's something wrong with girls who have small bottoms either, and just to be clear there's nothing wrong with boys who like other boys' bottoms, just that they're probably not the sort of boys who'd be interested in a red-blooded vixen like yourself. Did I dig myself out there OK?

Anyway, to help you visualize how insignificant this 'problem' is, I've done a bar chart.

Love

Miss Understanding

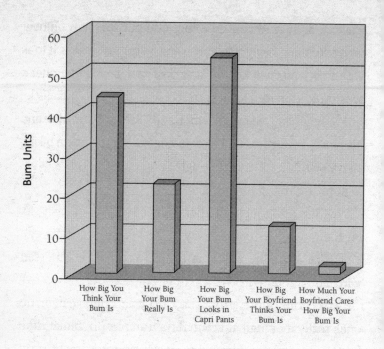

Bum Units

| How Big You Think Your Bum Is | How Big Your Bum Really Is | How Big Your Bum Looks in Capri Pants | How Big Your Boyfriend Thinks Your Bum Is | How Much Your Boyfriend Cares How Big Your Bum Is |

Staff Watch. Did anyone else notice a certain red-haired member of the Science department look very tired on Friday morning? Could this have anything to do with Third-off Thursday at Zeon? And said teacher has been observed spending a lot of time texting moodily whilst invigilating at the mocks. Could there be a love split? Or more likely a love triangle? Watch this space . . .

Email to crumpet83@notmail.com
Hey Crumpet
So I had my date with Al on the weekend. He's asked me

not to talk about it on the blog, which I agreed to. But I can tell you.

I think it went quite well really. Though you can never be sure with boys, can you? He has this nervous little laugh which he does whenever he says anything supposed to be funny. It started off pretty annoying but then I started to like it. Though I could just as quickly go back to finding it annoying.

We didn't do much; neither of us have a lot of cash, so we got a torpedo from Subway in the high street and went to the park cos it was such a nice day on Sunday. We watched the skateboarders pull down a wooden fence so they could build a ramp, until a man from the council came round to shout at them and they took photos of him on their mobiles. Which I'm ashamed to say we both found very funny.

Al's *quite* good at just general chatting. Boys aren't usually very good at it *at all*, and you know me, I can't keep my mouth shut even when I'm normal. So when I'm a bit nervous it's like there's an invisible magician pulling words out of my mouth like streams of coloured ribbons.

You asked on the phone the other day whether I fancy him? Dunno really. He's not really good-looking like Seth, or sexy like The Boy. He's maybe a bit too nice to be that attractive. But he's definitely not a minger. He looks like every other boy at Woodyatt this year. Gangly, a bit spotty, too much hair and jeans down round his knees.

He likes a band called Cogent which I said sounded like a team name from *The Apprentice*. I think he chose them because I wasn't likely to have heard of them. You know what boys are like; they want to know about stuff that you don't. I remembered that tip you gave me, pretend like you don't know *anything* and boys will just lap it up and start showing off.

Him: 'Did you know the earth goes around the sun, and not the other way around?'

Me: 'Shut UP! It so does not!'

Him: 'Did you know there have been seven James Bonds?'

Me: 'You *kidder*. Really?'

Him: 'Yes, George Lazenby is the one most people forget.'

Me: 'Wow, that's amazing, what's that building over there?'

Him: 'What that one? That's where they make salt.'

I'm really not sure I can keep up the dumb-act for long, and beside, I think he could tell I was putting it on. He kept laughing. Anyway, it's all hypothetical really, because he hasn't called me or texted or emailed since then, so maybe he's not interested.

Not that I care.

Luvs

An

Email from Crumpet@notmail.com

Wassa' Ans

Erm, do you think maybe him not contacting you might have something to do with your revelations about a certain Badboy in your last blog?

Gulp

Crumps

Email from Anya@Missunderstanding.net

Hey Crumps.

Bollocks. I didn't think of that.

An

Miss Understanding's
Christmas 2009 Special

Sorry about the long pause, like the polar bear said to the nail technician. I've been busy with Christmas which could best be described so far as an Utter Fiasco™. First of all Jocasta had forgotten she'd agreed to send out five hundred begging-letters for her charity, so she made me and Marley sit and help her stuff and lick the damn things. It took hours.

'Make a game out of it,' she said when we complained.

'Like how many we can lick before we throw up?' Marley asked, swollen-tongued.

'Or how many we can lick before I commit murder,' I suggested. 'Or shove them up your—'

'Darling!' said Jocasta to my brother. 'Why don't you go and get us all some chocolate from the fridge? There's some hidden under the lettuce. We can each have one square for every twenty-five envelopes we complete.'

She's cunning, my mother, I'll give her that. I blame that damn *Parent Power!* book she treats like a bible. If I ever find where she hides it, I'll burn it. Then we'll see who's boss round here. In the meantime I'll eat her chocolate I suppose.

Anyway, Christmas Day itself got off to a typical start when the tree fell over, crushing Marley. Mind you, it was his fault really; he should never have tried to climb it wearing Mum's novelty reindeer slippers. After we got that sorted out and tweezered the pine needles out of his back, we settled down to open our presents.

Mum had got me a yoga mat.

'Thanks,' I said, not meaning it.

'Now you can do your own mantra,' she said, enthusiastically.

'Thanks,' I said again. *Really* not meaning it.

I know she's not got money to burn, but if she's going to give me something crap, at least she could have made it a crap alternative to something I wanted. Like a Primani knock-off handbag. Or a fake Rolex, or Katie Price's new perfume.

I'd pre-empted her this year and had got her something equally crappy. A CD I'd burned (well, that Marley had burned for me) which was basically just my iPod top twenty-five playlist. I knew she wouldn't bother listening to it – she assumes anything I like, or that I think *she* might like would be rubbish. I sometimes find myself listening to something on shuffle and thinking: What is THIS crap? and it turns out it's an album I've just bought and have been recommending to everyone I know. Even worse is when I hear something I like and I think: What's this? This is great, and I look at the screen and realize it's the *High School Musical* soundtrack I downloaded for Marley to listen to on the way to Devon.

'Thanks,' Mum said and gave me a kiss. Then she went and poured herself a glass of wine. It was 11.15 am.

'It's Christmas,' she said when she saw my look. 'Do you want one?'

'Maybe with lunch,' I said.

Marley got the third gen Wii Plus he'd wanted. It is understood that all the money on the planet is spent on Marley at times like this and none at all on us. He was beside himself with glee for an hour until he found he couldn't get past the boss on level two of *Bloodclot Zombie III* and had a paddy. I had to do it for him.

'See,' I said, 'you should use the single barrel shotgun for greater accuracy. You need to hit him between the breastplates, see the bloody gobbets of flesh fly?'

Mum sat watching in horror, she rarely pays much attention to the violence and gore Marley spends most of his waking life immersed in. Being Christmas, she'd decided to 'get involved' and that meant trying to get her forty-six-year-old head around the control panel.

'It used to just be a joystick with one orange button,' Mum said, looking at the boomerang-shaped controller. 'This thing has more buttons on it than my car dashboard.'

'Well you do drive a 2CV,' I pointed out. 'Look, those buttons are the joystick, and that one's fire. Don't worry about the rest. I'll put it on tournament mode so you and Marley can slaughter each other while I get on with the turkey.'

Mum looked at me sharply. 'Turkey?' she squawked, sounding a little like one. Over her shoulder I saw Marley's on-screen character sneak up on her resting avatar and hack off its head with a pole-axe.

'Oh sorry, I forgot. I thought this was Christmas for a second. Silly me, now I remember it's Gluten-Free-Vegetarian Day. The day when the ghost of Linda McCartney slides down the Aga ventilation pipe and drops turd-like fake sausages in the nut roast.'

'You can eat meat if you like darling,' Mum said, peering at me over her glasses, 'just not in this house.' She turned back to the game. 'Now, who am I killing again?'

I left them shrieking and uttering oaths and went into the kitchen to make the nut roast. I don't mind nut roast really. It tastes OK if you crumble a beef stock cube all over it before cooking. When I came back into the living room I saw Mum's avatar had strapped Marley's to a table and was busily disembowelling it while he wrestled uselessly with the controls. She cackled and took a slug of wine. I rolled my eyes and came up to check my emails. How comforting that other people's disastrous social lives continue to go wrong over the holiday period.

Dear Miss Understanding

How do I know when I'm in love? The reason I ask is that I've been going out with this girl for a few weeks and, don't get me wrong, I really like her. She's really pretty and when she asked me out I was all like yippee but now what I feel isn't what they talk about in films. I don't get all hot and sweaty when she comes in the room, I don't lie in bed thinking about her and the other day I hadn't seen her for a week and she says, 'Did you miss me?' and I thought, like umm, not really.

I think it should be better than this.

Yours

Bodge

Dear Bodge

Yes, I think it should be better than this too. Maybe part of the problem is that she asked you out rather than the other way around. Now here at Missunderstanding.net we're all totally on board with the whole sexual equality scenario, no issues there. But still, there's something nice about the tradition of the man asking the woman out. Don't you think? I wonder if you feel emasculated on a subconscious level? Or maybe it's that you lacked the thrill of the chase, and the urgency that comes from fear of rejection.

Here's the test. Imagine her snogging your best friend. Does that make you feel like you want to punch him and throw his X-box out the window? Or do you find the thought about as interesting as a cricket match tea break?

I think we both know the answer. Both of you deserve much more. Break up with this girl before you both die of boredom.

Yours

Miss more-in-sadness-than-anger Understanding

Dear Miss Understanding

First let me just explain that I'm not a student at your school. I'm a little older than your usual correspondents but I've been following your blog with interest over the last few months. I enjoy it very much.

I'm writing with a problem of my own. My problem is that I'm a love cheat. There, I've said it. I'm seeing two men at once. It started quite innocently, I made a date with a man, and before that date came around, a new man started at my work and he asked me out as well. I wasn't sure about either of them at first so didn't see any harm in going on both dates.

Things have become serious in a romantic sense, now I can't choose between them. Maybe you can help?

One of the men is very wealthy, though quite a lot older than I am. Let's call him Max. Knowing you, you'll want to know exactly how wealthy and how old, well let's just say he has all his own teeth and keeps them in a vault in Switzerland.

The other guy, let's call him Josh, is more my age, and he's better-looking if I'm to be honest. He's funny and sweet and I think he should be the one, for those reasons. But Max has a certain something that Josh doesn't. Maybe it's experience. He has a look that he gives me that just makes me melt. He's a man, not a boy.

My head says Josh, but my heart wants Max. I think.

Please help!

Barrelgirl

Dear Barrelgirl

Ooh babe, you've got it bad. I feel for you, having some experience with older men myself (search for The Boy in previous blog entries). I think this is going to take all my skills to help you through this one.

I need more information. Particularly about Josh. There must be something about him, something more than smooth skin and a tight backside; otherwise you would have just chosen Max.

   Yours

   MU

OK, I finally got the 411 on the Jugs/Poop-chute situation. I had to call Crumpet in the end, which is not ideal, because she's so vacant and so pretty she doesn't know who *she's* going out with half the time, let alone anyone else. She's also a half-story type of person. She'll tell you something interesting she read in the paper, but forget some critical piece of information. Like she might say, 'Vernon Kay was hit by a car yesterday.' 'Oh my God,' you'll say, 'is he OK?' 'Hmmm?' she'll answer. 'I don't know, I didn't pay much attention to that bit, I was distracted by a picture of a monkey riding a dog.'

   Or when that bloke was attacked by a shark in Australia and fought it off with a biro. 'Where did he get the biro?' I'll say. 'I don't know, I didn't read to the end,' she'll reply. 'Maybe he was doing Sudoku on a lilo?'

   So anyway, true to form, Crumpet has picked up that they've split because one of them snogged someone else, but she doesn't know which one! All she knows is that Jugs no longer goes down to the Bull and has formed a breakaway group at the Fox, which is pretty radical news, because she told me she wouldn't ever set foot in that place again after someone saw *Gordon Ramsay's Kitchen Nightmares* researchers sniffing about last year.

This is so frustrating. I need information. Actually, I need to get back to Clifton. Have concocted a cunning plan. I'll take Cheryl up on her invitation, and suggest I go over for the weekend. I can go over Friday night, heal the Jugs/Poop-chute rift. Stay for dinner on Saturday and come back Sunday. Mum can spend that time re-acquainting herself with the Aga. Though it's more likely that I'll end up preparing a vat of veggie cottage pie they can reheat.

Yours glumly

Miss Understanding

Later on Christmas Day:

Been having a bit of Mum's wine. And some sherry truffles. I'll warn you, I'm a bit drunkie-poos. Not my fault, and don't say I didn't warn you. Made the mistake of reading some of Mum's magazines and just wanted to share with you what a bunch of stinkers blokes are. Also sent HAPPY CHRISTMAS XXX to The Boy and after three hours of textpectation got zilcho to show for it.

Now, I read in a serious magazine (Dunhill adverts and everything) that there are only ten per cent of men who NEVER lie, and who NEVER cheat. Now I have no actual evidence with which to back up the following theory, but I reckon most of that ten per cent look like one of the following:

1) Phil Mitchell off *EastEnders*
2) The fat one from Westlife
3) Phillip Schofield off *This Morning*
4) Gordon Brown
5) Prince Charles (maybe he's not a good example cos he *did* cheat, but he *is* the heir to the throne and can do what he wants so in my view he's the exception that proves the rule).

So basically what this means is that anyone you even half fancy is almost certainly going to cheat on you. Either get used to it, or get your geek on and start sexting with Fat Gareth.

But before you reach for that Nokia, wait, there's more. If I turn to the cheaper, yet more entertaining magazine to my left (adverts mostly for sanitary products), I discover the two following separate, yet interlinked statistics: twenty-five per cent of men admit to having cheated on their girlfriends and ninety per cent of men are compulsive liars. That makes one hundred and fifteen per cent! Extraordinary. What rats men are! This suggests to me that one hundred per cent of men have a bit on the side, and fifteen per cent of them have a bit on the side of the bit on the side.

Even Fat Gareth! Though he has so many sides

he probably makes up a good twenty per cent of the fifteen per cent.

Oh hell, now I'm confused, maybe I should do a chart. No I know what, I need to go back down and eat a nut-roast sandwich. I think we all can agree though. Men are no good!

MU

PS Happy Christmas.

Email to Jugs93@btinterweb.com

Hey babe

Crumps told me you and Poops broke up. She was sketchy on the details, so I completely will not believe that until I hear it from you. But the fact you have your phone on voice suggests that is what has happened. You're my BFF though Jugs, so no way will I talk to Poop about this until I've talked to you first, please call soon. Or if not, then email or SMS is fine.

I love you honey and hope you're OK.

Miss you

Anya

Email to Poop_chute@notmail.com

Poops! What's going on man? Crumpet gave me the news. No one's talking to me. I feel bereft here, buddy, bereft. Jugs won't return my calls. Throw me a frickin' bone!

Love Anya

PS hope you're OK, and all that. Me, I've got this bad knee thing I was telling you about, and I feel like I'm getting mumps again. Or maybe it's lymphatic cancer?

Email from Poop_chute@notmail.com
Hey Buxton,

Yes, it's all true I'm afraid. Sorry I didn't call. I kind of thought you'd be in Jugs's camp y'know. At times like this it's not just the CDs that get divided. (Not that Jugs and I have a joint CD collection but you get me.)

When are you coming to visit us poor mountain folk? I'll ask you kindly to leave your big-town airs and graces behind though. The Boy and I are at the Bull if you're around on Friday. I heard Jugs is hanging out at the Fox so would understand if you went there instead.

Cheers

Px

PS I'm OK, though have dislocated my collarbone, had a leg off and also developed this weird sniffle that pops up from time to time, usually when I'm thinking about this dark-haired girl I used to know. Am treating it with beer, which seems to help.

Email to Jugs93@btinterweb.com

Hey sweetie

I'm getting worried now. Look forward to hearing from you.

Love

Anya

Miss Understanding Blog Entry
– 8th January 2010

Dear Miss Understanding

I've been sort of seeing this older guy from Kyoto over the internet. We have webcams and we just chat and flirt and stuff. We're both into Manga you see, so I reckon he's probably OK. He said maybe he might come to England soon probably. Anyway last night he asked me to maybe take my top off and I just froze and switched off the Mac, I was so shocked. But I've been thinking that maybe it would probably be all right? It's only on a webcam and it's probably just fun isn't it?

Do you think I should maybe take my top off?

Yours

Fweffadf;kj

Dear Fweffadf;kj

Hmmm, probably I think maybe, that you maybe

probably should maybe keep your top firmly maybe definitely *on*!

What on earth makes you think that this guy is probably OK because he's interested in Manga? Does Manga necessarily make people gentle and supportive and non-creepy? I think not, my friend.

How old is this guy anyway? I strongly recommend you block him and stop talking to weird dudes on the net. Here, I googled a link to a Manga convention in London next week. Go there, find a real boy and talk to him at length about violent and misogynistic graphic novels.

Next!

Miss   Understanding-all-too-well-the-dangers-of-the-internet

Email from <u>Anya.Buxton@notmail.com</u>
To: J_Buxton@clayjones.co.uk
Dear Dad

I don't want you to think I'm telling tales or anything, but you'll never guess what Mum's been getting up to. She's started this new course in Shinjugu. I thought it was a suburb of Tokyo, but apparently it's an ancient form of meditation/self-defence that's recently been discovered by historio-linguists who have used super-computers to crack a code that's stumped the world's best cryptographers for a thousand years. And that's a direct quote from the *Mail on Sunday*.

Apparently the practice of this form of meditation is restricted to those who have achieved Acolyte status in this Cult, er, sorry, Discipline. No Untutored Ones must Witness the Solemn Rituals (though from tedious past experience with Mum's meditative exercises I suspect they involve humming softly, moving your arms around and twisting gently, like a slowed-down version of John Travolta in *Pulp Fiction*).

All of which means, basically, that Marley and I got turfed out and weren't able to watch *The Apprentice* last night, which excluded me from ninety per cent of the Oh-my-God-did-you-see-it-last-night conversation at Woodyatt. It's hard enough making friends as it is, without being stripped of all cultural references.

This new-age thing is getting worse, I'm sure of it. I know you said that it was just a phase she was going through to get her over the divorce. But that was two years ago! I'm not saying it was nothing, but I'm not convinced she was really that cut up about it tell the truth. It was worse for me and Marley, when it led to the family breaking up. (And yes I know it's all for the best, I know this isn't Disney. I so don't have some childish plan to try and get you and Mum back together – perish the thought.

Anyway, I was wondering whether you could have another talk with her about the Sky Plus situation. It's hypocritical of her to be ideologically opposed to pay television only to then continually ask Marley to set up the stone age VHS recorder to tape *Deal or No Deal* on yoga night.

And that's another thing, Dad. Marley's behaviour is getting worse. Mum made the mistake of asking him to fix her computer when she dropped cooked bulgur wheat into the DVD slot (I honestly don't know). He did fix it, but in a way that means only he is able to turn it on and off. So every time Mum wants to fire it up she has to ask him to help, which, after extensive and detailed negotiations between the two of them he's only agreed to do if each time she lets him illegally download an episode of *South Park*, which is wrong on so many levels I don't know where to start.

I confronted Mum about it and she pulled out her *Parent Power!* book and showed me the chapter titled 'They're not Bribes, They're Rewards'. I pointed out it wasn't so much a reward as a blackmail payment, but she laughed and told me I had a lot to learn about children. Now I just leave her to it.

She's not tough enough on him, Dad. I'm not saying you were the scariest father in the world; Crumpet's dad once punched a hole in her door when she locked herself in during an argument – that's scary! But you used to tell us off all the time. Mum hardly ever said anything, and now you're gone, well she's given up altogether. Someone needs to yell at us from time to time.

Also, he's waking in the night. I was woken at 3.07 in the morning on Tuesday with him playing *Guitar Hero 4* at top volume. I put earplugs in but it was no good. He seems to have a mental block and can't get past level three for some reason, so I had to get up and play the entire set at Glastonbury to help him out. Some have greatness thrust upon them . . .

Anyway, maybe we can discuss when I come over for dinner? Please thank Cheryl again for her invitation and no, I am not a pescatarian, regardless of what my mother says on the matter.

Love

Anya

Dear Parent,

It has come to our attention that a student at Adam Woodyatt Academy has established a 'blog' site upon which she dispenses irresponsible advice to fellow members of the student body. This student had previously been an anonymous contributor to the school webzine and goes by the name Miss Understanding.

Ordinarily, the staff at Adam Woodyatt Academy would

not interfere with a student's private and extra-curricular activities, but the blog also contains frequent, offensive references to members of staff which many feel to be an invasion of privacy. There is also the matter of the glib and potentially harmful advice being given out. The blog is, I am afraid to say, extremely popular.

This student has revealed numerous clues to her identity via her blog, but due to the restrictions of the data protection act, amendment 3viii clause 2b (2002), we cannot use the school database to identify this student, though we have our suspicions. We would appreciate assistance in tracking this student down so we can discuss with her the potential dangerous ramifications of her activities and try to help her put her obvious creativity and writing ability to better use.

Please contact the school on <u>woodyatt@notmail.com</u>. All correspondence will be in the strictest confidence.

Yours sincerely

Tim Grafton

Head Teacher

Adam Woodyatt Academy

Miss Understanding Blog Entry
– 12th January 2010

They're coming to get me! I'm scared, Woodyatt, I'm so scared.

How funny though that they can't simply cross-reference the obvious hints I keep dropping with the information they hold about my family. Obviously Jocasta and Marley aren't my mother and brother's real names but still, it shouldn't take the Spooks team to get to the bottom of this.

Ah, fuggedaboudit. They'll find me eventually, but what are they gonna do? I have other problems just at the moment anyway, you guys all seem to hate me too!

I received huge amounts of mail after last week's column, mostly about my advice to poor old Bodge, flailing weakly in a loveless relationship. Apparently my revelation that I'm a bit of a traditionalist got some of you angrier than Naomi Campbell on a budget flight to New York.

Do I feel put in my place or what? Bubbles Gosling writes: 'This isn't 1994, did the Spice Girls mean nothing to you?' Erica Bainbridge pointed out that she asked her boyfriend out first, he said no, and then changed his mind and they've now 'been together for nearly a year and are totally happy'. Whatever.

'There's an entire chapter in Germaine Greer's *The Female Eunuch* about girls like you,' says Bonny Greaves, abandoning Gossipbitch.com for a few minutes to fire a broadside at me.

Even worse, the alpha-males are writing in with entirely unwanted support, which is like Robert Mugabe saying he likes your ideas on electoral reform. 'About time someone took a stand against feminism,' bleats Guy DuLancey. 'Relationships work best when theirs (sic) a strong man and a pretty girl.'

Which is not what I was saying at all, talk about misunderstandings. Look, let me provide some clarification here (I know I sound like a politician caught lying). All I meant was that it's difficult for boys these days. We live in the future now and girls aren't repressed any more, we're not expected to spend our lives just looking after men like we used to. We're all sassy and confident and kick-ass these days. We're doing better than boys at school too. I just think that boys sometimes don't know what they're for. In the past the boy used to do the first bit, and then the girl would take over and do the difficult stuff, like having kids. If girls are now taking control of even the asking-out bit, then it's natural that some boys may feel a bit, well useless, really . . .

Anyway, I'll let it go. I don't want this to come between us. Sheesh. I wish I hadn't said anything now. A good magician knows how to redirect the audience; I'll post three of the most agonizing problems I've yet seen to help take your minds off how much you all want to burn my bra. With me in it.

Dear Miss Unders

I think I might be gay, innit. I was staying at my mate's house and we had to share his bed and when I wake up I've got my arm around him and I'm all like hard and that.

What should I do? I totally don't want to bum him. Or anyone. Not a bloke anyway. I can't sleep.

Help me.

Blud

Dear Blud

Basically the answer is don't worry about it. You may be gay, you may not. My research tells me it's common for young men, or young women, to fool around with each other. It's just your sexuality poking its head out from under the leaves, having a look about and wondering which way to go. And who wouldn't have a little cuddle with a nice warm body lying next to them while they sleep?

One time when my friend Becca stayed over, I woke in the morning to find her hand was . . . actually come to think of it, never you mind where her hand was, the point is that it didn't mean anything.

Whether you're gay or not, always remember that you don't have to do anything you don't want, with anyone you don't like. If you don't want to sleep with men, then don't. That choice is yours to make and yours alone.

Personally I'd advise you to keep an open mind. Don't be too rigid. As it were.

Stay cool

Miss Understanding

Dear Miss Understanding
Can you get pregnant the first time you do it unprotected?
Best
Curious

Dear Curious,
Hmmm. Let me flick through my extensive literature on the subject. Oh look at that, turns out you can. Oh and while we're on it, you can get pregnant the first time you do it *protected* as well. Less likely, but still possible.

Bear it in mind.

Miss U

Dear Miss Understanding

A friend of mine has an embarrassing problem. She was given a credit card by her parents to use in emergencies and she's used it sometimes when there wasn't so much of an emergency, unless you count not having the right shoes an emergency.

She owes £1,346.73 and earns £45.50 a week from her part-time job at Waitrose. Her parents will totally kill her if they find out. What the hell should my friend do?

Yours

Ms Worried

Dear Worried

Just as well for me 'your friend' was so open with you about the exact situation. Some 'friends' would have been totally vague about the sums involved. It's a good sign, as is your decision to write in to me. You're . . . I mean your friend is A) willing to admit she has a problem B) prepared to seek help and C) possessed of the brains to keep track of her incomings and outgoings.

Here's what to do. First, cut up the card. Second, get down to your bank. Tell them the problem. Tell them how much is owed and how much you earn. Agree a repayment plan with them. Third, stick to this for six weeks. Fourth, tell your parents what you did and what you're doing to get yourself out of it.

I'm pretty sure they won't kill you. If they do, then they'll have to pay back the loan themselves. So it's win-win, right?

Luv

Miss Understanding

Now. I'm going to be a bit naughty here. Do you lot remember Al? The guy who asked me out on a date via the blog? Well I saw him again last night, and he didn't specifically say I couldn't write about this date on the blog. What he *did* say was that he was going to stop reading the blog altogether.

'Just because you have no respect for your own privacy, doesn't mean I want to know every detail about your life,' he said.

He didn't raise the subject of what I'd written about The Boy, so either he hasn't read it or that's the reason he says he's stopping reading, so he can avoid discussing it completely.

Either way, I guess this means I'm clear to tell you all what happened. So here goes.

First of all he turned up with his dad, which was a bit random. I looked over Al's shoulder towards the car, where I could see his dad tapping the wheel in time to Radio 2.

'Is he some kind of chaperone?' I asked.

'Eh? Oh no, he's driving us to the restaurant.'

'Is he eating with us? Because he's not having any of my garlic bread.'

'No, nothing like that,' Al said.

'OK, fair enough.'

But then Mum had appeared as if from nowhere. She was wearing her new glasses and one of Dad's old macintoshes and looked a bit Special Needs to be honest.

'Hello darling, is this your boyfriend?'

Al reddened instantly. I was too embarrassed for him to be embarrassed for myself, besides, I'm used to it.

'No Mum, this is Al – he and I are just going out for a pizza.'

'Would you like to come in for ten minutes?' Mum said, apparently fascinated by him.

'Erm, I'm sorry, I have my dad in the car,' Al said.

Mum seemed to find this a bit random and immediately lurched towards the car, evidently intent on quizzing this strange man as to where he was taking her daughter. 'I'll go and say hello,' I heard her mutter as she shuffled off in her slippers, leaving a trail through the wet grass of the front lawn.

She tapped on the driver's window, giving Al's dad the

fright of his life. Probably he thought she was a lunatic, or possibly a dogger. 'Hello!' I heard her cry through the window. 'I'm Jocasta.' He wound down the window and they immediately started up an intense discussion about how difficult teenagers are and what do we think they are, a taxi service? Etc etc. Why don't adults have any conversation?

'Sorry about this,' Al and I said to each other at exactly the same time. Then we laughed.

We finally set off, after promising Jocasta I'd be back by 11.00 pm. The car journey was a little awkward at first with no one talking, but then Mr Al started asking me questions. He'd obviously been primed by Mrs Al. 'Find out more about this girl, is she rough? Is she on drugs? What on earth does she see in Al?' That sort of thing.

'So,' he said. 'What do you . . . what do you normally get up to on the weekends?'

'Crystal meth,' I mumbled. Al giggled next to me.

'What?'

'History and Maths,' I said, louder. 'Revision, you know?'

'Oh, and how long have you lived in Allerton?'

'Since September.'

'Do you like it?'

'Yes,' I lied.

Mr Al drove us to the central car park and parked. As we got out and thanked him for the ride, I saw him take a thermos and packet of sandwiches out of a bag, then settle back in his seat.

'He's going to wait for us?' I said incredulously as we walked off.

'Hmmm? Oh yes,' Al said. 'He likes it; he says it's the only peace and quiet he ever gets.'

'It's not so he can keep an eye on you then?'

'Shouldn't think so, I have four younger sisters. Sitting in the car alone is what he lives for these days.'

'I never want to get old,' I said.

The meal went OK. We talked about music mostly. Or at least he named bands and I said 'never heard of them'. Then I'd name a band, and he'd wince. He got us a bottle of wine (they didn't even ID him) which I thought was quite sophisticated really, even if I only had a glass – I think he was hoping I'd have more and let myself go.

He had a coffee and I had tiramisu which is bound to have bypassed my stomach altogether and gone straight for my thighs. After he'd paid (I offered!), he asked me if I'd like to walk for a while before we went back to the car.

'How romantic,' I said. 'I don't often get a chance to promenade before I'm taken to the car park.'

'I don't know whether to take you seriously sometimes,' he said.

'I may not always be serious,' I admitted. 'But you should certainly always take me serious-ly.'

He was still puzzling over this as I led the way out and down towards Bridewell St.

'Hey,' he said eventually, 'do you know Bubbles Gosling?'

'Not really, she sometimes writes to Miss Understanding.'

'Well she's friends with my older sister.'

'Right.'

'Right, well, I was talking to her about you, about how you didn't have any . . . I mean how you didn't really know anyone in Allerton, and she said to get your number and she'd invite you to a DVD night they're having next week.'

I stopped walking. 'Is that how everyone sees me then, as some Nigella-no-friends needing chum-charity?'

'No,' he protested, horrified. 'I didn't mean that. It's just that you don't really talk to anyone and people think you're a bit . . .'

'A bit what?'

'Well a bit aloof.'

'Stuck-up.'

'I didn't say that.'

'But some people do? Well, screw them.' I started walking again, this time faster. 'Did it occur to you that I might not *need* friends? Especially ones called Bubbles.'

'You might not need them, but they're nice to have,' he said.

'I have friends, in Clifton,' I pointed out.

'You live here now.'

'Can we talk about something else?'

'Of course,' he said, relieved.

'I mean, thanks for thinking of me,' I said, hoping I hadn't broken him already. 'But really, I'm OK.'

We went back to chatting about popular culture. Movies this time. He likes foreign films (or so he claimed). I told him I liked Hollywood blockbusters and, rom-coms. To be honest, I might have overdone it about just how shallow my taste is, but I had to shut him up about Pedro Almodovar, who's made a bunch of films about Spanish transvestites and nuns . . . and sex . . . as far as I can see. Al was doing his best to persuade me to get *Habla Con Ella* out on DVD, but I wasn't having any.

Still, everything was going fine as we walked down the high street, the streetlights reflecting romantically off the smashed alcopop bottles in the gutter, and I started wondering if he was going to try and hold my hand, which I might not have minded so much. Then he stopped and turned to face me. First he looked around, presumably to check if his dad was sneaking about in the shadows like Gollum. Then the next thing I knew he was kissing me. He put his arms around my back and though I was a little shocked, it was really quite nice. Thing is, I could feel him fiddling about round the back. I wasn't sure what he was up to but it was quite distracting, especially when I felt my wrap-around shoulder bag come loose and fall to the ground. He'd undone the catch.

'Are you trying to steal my purse?' I asked.

'What?'

'Cos it would have been an extremely long-winded hustle,' I went on. 'And hardly worth the time, unless you know a receiver of stolen tampons?'

'I was just trying to take your bra off. That's all.' He bent to pick up the bag and tried to fix the strap.

I tried not to laugh. 'Why are you trying to take off my bra outside Millets?' I asked. 'What were you planning to do once you'd got it off?'

He shrugged. 'I don't know. It's just what boys do, isn't it?'

'Right, like kneeing blokes in the nuts is just what girls do.'

And if he tries to remove my bra *or* my bag again, he may find himself singing falsetto for a week or so.

Long time

Miss Understanding

Miss Understanding Blog Entry
– 22nd January 2010

OH. MY. GOD! I had such a row with Mum last night. It all started when she came into my room and tried to make conversation. I could tell she was curious about something.

'Hello sweetie, I'm popping into Boots tomorrow and just wondered if you wanted me to get anything.'

I recognized this as a trick she'd learnt from *Parent Power!* Not being five, I didn't fall for it.

'Like what?' I said, innocently.

'Well, do you need tampons? Or chap-stick?'

'No thanks, I'm fine for those.'

'What about condoms?' she asked, watching me closely.

I opened my dresser drawer and looked inside. 'Er, yes, all right, get me some condoms please. Extra-large and ribbed for her pleasure . . . I mean *my* pleasure.'

Mum looked like she'd been shot. 'I . . . I . . .' she stuttered.

'Well as you're endorsing teenage sex now, I'd better prepare myself,' I went on.

'I am not endorsing teenage sex!' she said hurriedly.

'Buying me condoms is hardly *dis*couraging it.'

'I was just asking because I wanted to know if you were using them.'

'Oh I seeeeeee,' I said. 'You were trying to trick me, mother.'

She eyed me up and down. 'You're joking,' she said. 'You're not having sex at all.'

I smiled. Time to put her out of her misery. 'I'm not using condoms, Mum, no.'

'Thank heavens for that,' she said, visibly deflating with relief.

'So if you are really going to Boots, could you get me a pregnancy test?' I said.

'Don't push it,' she growled.

Now that was all fine. We were teasing each other, circling like cats, but we got through it and that would have been the perfect time for her to walk away and leave things alone. But she couldn't. She had to take the opportunity to start up on something else.

'This isn't like you, darling,' Mum said, looking around at the post-Glastonbury-style chaos. 'Your room is so messy.'

'It's not politically correct to say my room is messy,' I replied. 'You should say it's otherly-organized, or alternately-neat.'

'Don't be flippant, darling. I'd like you to tidy your room please.'

This is what annoys me. I'm the one who does all the bloody cleaning in that house. My room is the only place I don't clean. Because it's my room and I can do what I want there. I accept my responsibilities in the rest of the house, to cook and clean up after Marley the Prodigal Wolverine and She Who Must be Humoured.

I nearly refused but then remembered I needed her permission to go and stay with Dad and Cheryl on the weekend. 'Yeah, OK,' I said.

'Thanks,' she said, and smiled at me.

'Mum,' I said, as she turned to go. 'Cheryl and Dad have asked me if I can go to theirs for dinner on Saturday.' This was a total lie of course, we hadn't agreed on a date, but if you wait around for invitations in this world you end up on the Z-list. Just turn up and sparkle, darling.

She stopped, her face turned away from me and slightly hidden by the door frame.

'Oh . . .' she said.

'And also Jugs has broken up with Poop-ch . . . um, Peter, and so I was hoping to maybe catch up with her too, so I was thinking if I could go—'

'The thing is,' Mum said, coming back into view, 'that I need you to look after Marley on Saturday. I have my Reiki, then I have Shinjugu.'

I just stared at her.

'Darling, don't look at me like that.'

'Can't you get someone else to baby-sit? I've got a life too, you know!'

'It is rather short notice, sweetie. I'm happy for you to go out on Friday night, and on Saturday night too, but can't you go out in Allerton? With your friends here? I can't have you away all weekend.'

And then I just lost it. 'I don't *have* any bloody friends here!' I yelled. 'I spend all my free time cooking and cleaning for your son.'

Then she put on that calm quiet voice they told her to use in parenting classes, like I'm some kind of axe-wielding lunatic. She hooked her frizzy hair back over her ears, which is the signal that lets me know she's angry.

'Anya, I think you need to calm down and have a think about what you've just said.' She took a deep breath and held my eye. 'I'm going downstairs now. You can come down when you're ready to apologize.' Then she left.

Well, I'm not saying sorry. She's got more chance of getting an apology from Guy Ritchie for making *Revolver*. I'm going to Clifton tomorrow night whatever she says. She'll just have to cancel bloody Reiki. My friends need me!

* * *

I hope you don't think I'm neglecting *you* though, my lovely Woodyatt-folk? You don't think I care more about my dumb friends in Clifton? Don't be like that. It's just that I'm quite new in this town, I don't have many friends here, which I guess is how come none of you (apart from one confused young lad) seem to have figured out who I am, despite all the heavy clues I've been dropping.

Here are some of your emails, just to prove I still love you.

(via text)

DEAR MISS UNDERSTANDING

OK, SOS I AKSED THIS GIRL OUT LIKE YOU SEZ AND WE WENT 2 MACD'S. IT WOZ GD BUTT I COULD NOT THINK OF WHAT TO SAY 2 HER. WE WENT 2 ZEON AFTER AND SOME OF HER M8S WAS THERE AND SHE TALKED TO THEM AND I TALKED TO MY MATES AND ME SEZ GOODBYE AT THE END BUT THEN THAT'S IT AND ME WENT HOME AND I'M NOT SURE IF IT WENT OK.

WOT DO U FINK?

GEX

Dear Gex

Well it doesn't sound like my ideal evening, but then I have this glamorous image of myself as some kind of 1930s starlet deserving nothing short of champagne cocktails and a convertible-ride along a beach. Seriously, for a first date it doesn't sound so bad, but I think you need to step things up a bit now.

Tell her you had a nice time and aks her out again. This time go upmarket, take her to Supreme Burger and get the chilli fries. Zeon is fine cos it means you won't have to do none o' that talking stuff which, let's face it, is not your thing. Perhaps this time, though, you might actually dance with her?

Up to you of course.

Good luck

MU

Dear Miss Understanding

I'd give my boyfriend maybe an eight out of ten in most things. But when it comes to snogging he's about as sensitive as a devil dog. He always does the same thing, he starts off kissing all tender and that, but after about thirty seconds he starts breathing heavily and grabs my right boob.

He squeezed it so hard last night it gave me a bruise. 'It's not an avocado,' I said. But he just says he loses control with the passion of it all. Erica Bainbridge says all boys are the same, it's not top-half fumbling I need to worry about and that I'll be OK as long as I wear winter jeans.

What should I do? I feel he's spoiling something that should be really nice.

Yours

Frustrated

Dear Frustrated

Don't, for the love of your iPod, listen to Erica Bainbridge on this subject. I heard she's very willing to let boys grab hold of any bit they like as long as it's above the belt.

I say we girls need to stand firm against this sort of encroachment because a lot of boys are animals basically and they won't stop at the boobs. It'll be tummies next, then hips, then bottoms, then before you know it . . . well I don't think I need to spell it out, you can see as well as me where this is headed.

Just say no to hands.

So what *do* you do to make him stop crushing your baps like a baker who's lost his wedding ring? Well let me take a lesson from Mum's favourite book, *Parent Power!* Teenage boys are just little children with extra hormones, so we should treat them the same way. Rewards work better than punishments. So rather than slapping his hand away every time he reaches for the top-shelf, why not try hinting that you might let him have a little sneaky-peek at the little trouble-makers if he can keep his hands around your back (or his, if you think you can get away with it) for the entire session? You don't actually have to go through with the visual display if you don't want; girls are entitled to change their mind after all. Just start crying and say, 'I thought I could do it but I'm just not ready. Do you hate me?' You should be able to use this tactic, or variations on it, almost indefinitely. Boys aren't that smart really. You have what they want, therefore, you have power over the slobbering fools, be prepared to use it.

Love

Miss Understanding

Dear Miss Understanding

Tell me how much this sucks! I was on the PC the other night, not doing anything wrong, just downloading some music off of BitTorrent and I clicked back on the browser too many times and saw this site my dad must have been looking at. It was *Girlswithguns.com*, which is not at all what I'm into (though I was impressed by the way Suki handled the recoil on the Kalashnikov). Anyway, I'm checking it out, thinking what a weirdo my dad is when my mum comes in and sees what I'm looking at. What could I do? I can't tell her it was Dad, that's breaking the Dude's Code. So I had to take a bullet for him. Not cool.

Now she told Dad I was looking at violent porn, he gets

mad, then he realized what it was I was checking out, so he gives me this don't-tell-her look, and I was so embarrassed I wish I *had* been the one watching Marina test-firing the Glock semi-automatic.

So I get the talk about respecting women, and now I'm grounded, and I can't look my dad in the eye, and now I know why there's such a high suicide rate amongst young men in this country. They've all been busted for looking at their dad's porn collection.

I know there's not much you can do to help, but I'd appreciate your take on this. You always know what to say.

Yours

Red-faced Roy

Dear Roy

I feel for you. But what the hell is the Dude's Code? I don't know about this. Have you just let slip something that all men know about but which up until now no female has ever been made aware of?

If so, you're doubly in the poo now. Not only held in contempt by your mother, unable to face your father, you'll be an outcast, rejected by your own kind. You'll have to turn traitor and throw yourself on the mercy of the female species, buying our protection with further secrets from the Dude's Code.

You're right when you say I can't offer a simple solution

to sort this out for you. You've just got to wait it out. Eventually the embarrassment will fade. Every family's story is one of dull monotony punctuated by sharp points of hideous embarrassment, rage, or pain. Like in those Greek tragedies. They edit out the boring bits, you know. It wasn't all murdering your father and shagging your mum, there were long periods in between where they'd just sit about multi-slacking and eating hoola-hoops. If this is the worst you experience this year, you're in credit.

Families are about forgiveness and pretending you don't know that the others are nothing but walking sacs of human frailty, all held together with character flaws.

And just remember, if your old man is ever threatening you with all-out war, maybe he's gonna kick your butt, or throw you out, or forbid you from seeing some awful girl, you've always got the nuclear option of bringing up Marina and the Glock semi-automatic. And he knows it. Play the long game, Roy my friend. Play the looooong game.

Yours

Miss Understanding

Blue Sky Corner: After my recent ill-fated first date with Al. I wondered if there were others out there who've had bad first date experiences (not that mine was BAD as such, just amusing).

Write in and let me know your Worst Firsts.

Miss Understanding Blog Entry
– 24th February 2010

What a great day. Started off as usual with typical breakfast.

Marley: eating cereal containing two hundred per cent of his daily caffeine requirement whilst watching *Skins* on Mum's laptop.

Me: drinking Tetley and nibbling on white toast, flicking through *Sunday Times* review section whilst eying up Mum's copy of *Heat*.

Mum: sipping lapsang souchong with added extra organic cow manure, shovelling her home-made muesli into her face, a sunflower seed stuck firmly to her cheek.

'White bread gives you diabetes, darling,' she said, conversationally.

'Good,' I said, trying to shut her down.

'What's diabetes?' Marley asked.

'It's something you get when you eat too much white bread,' Mum said.

'How do you know if you've got it?' he asked, eyeing the toast rack.

'You fart a lot,' Mum said.

'Oh no,' he said, looking worried.

'Right,' I said, pushing my chair back. 'Well done, Mum. I think I've finished, I'm going to school.'

Before I left, I packed a bag. I'm not going back there tonight. In fact I'm writing this on the bus, on the way to Clifton. I phoned Dad on the way to school and asked him if I could stay the weekend. He said, 'Er, yes I suppose. I'll tell Cheryl.' So that was a relief.

There's a man next to me who keeps looking over my shoulder at what I'm writing. Hey you, Mr Nosey. You need a breath mint. Ha, that worked, he's looking out the window now. I feel a bit bad about the breath mint thing, he doesn't have bad breath, but there you go, no one crosses Miss Understanding.

Sorry about that, had to stop typing. The ride gets bumpy once you start going up the hill. Thought I'd better leave it till I got to Dad's. I'd texted him to say what bus I was on, and who did I find at the bus stop? Cheryl, in a BMW convertible. It was a little chilly to be driving round with the top down, but I think she was showing off a bit.

If I had a BMW convertible I'd have the top down too. Even in a blizzard.

I threw my bag in the back and we set off, shivering our way up the rest of the hill towards the Moonbase. Cheryl chattering away as she drove. 'I'm so excited you're here – and for the whole weekend. I'm really looking forward to getting to know you. Your father's working late tonight so I thought we girlies could veg out on the sofa with a pizza and some old episodes of *Sex and the City*.'

That did sound like fun actually, and I felt awful when I had to explain I was intending to spend the night with my mates down the pub. 'Sorry,' I said, 'I don't want it to seem like I'm using you as a crash pad for a drunken evening with my mates, I just thought it would be a good opportunity to catch up with my friends.'

'I think it's a brilliant idea, sweetie, you go out and enjoy yourself,' she said, not missing a beat, though I was watching her face as she drove and I thought for just a second that maybe she clenched her teeth slightly as she said it. I'd disappointed her already. Oh wells, I thought, disappointing people is what we teenagers do, better get used to it, Chezza.

We reached the house and Cheryl showed me to my room. As we walked up the stairs she said, 'I suppose you don't get much opportunity to go out when you're at your mum's.'

'Er, no, not really. When I'm not swamped with homework I'm usually babysitting,' I said.

She tutted. 'It's important for a girl to get away from the home from time to time,' she said. 'Let your hair down, go a little crazy.'

'Yes, I suppose,' I said, not sure about this. To be honest it never got very crazy down the Bull. We'd spend half the evenings counting shrapnel and trying to figure out whether we had enough for another round of lager tops, and the other half shouting out the wrong answers at people on the *Weakest Link* quiz machine..

I blinked in shock as I walked into the bedroom. 'Your room,' Cheryl said. It's amazing what you can do with a hundred square foot of floor and window space plus £6,000 to spend on soft furnishings. The bed alone is nearly bigger than my entire room in Allerton; you could fit half a dozen people in it. My bed at home is single and you'd struggle to get two in, unless they were Posh Spice and Nicole Ritchie, and even then they wouldn't get much sleep, what with all the sharp elbows.

'I'll drop you down the pub later on,' she said, 'after you've freshened up. Which one is it?'

And I had to stop and think. Where was I going to go? I had intended up until that moment to go to the Bull, because that was where we always went, that was the picture in my head of a happy time with all my mates. But it wasn't like that any more. Things had changed. Now Jugs would be at the Fox. Should I go there? I realized I'd been standing, staring at Cheryl, saying nothing.

'It's all right,' she said laughing, 'I'm not going to mate-crash. I just need to know where I'm taking you.' Oh hell, I thought. Maybe it was time to start being a bit more considerate to my host. 'Sorry!' I said. 'I'm not entirely sure where I'm going, it's quite a long story.'

'Do you have time for a quick bite before you go?' she asked. 'We could have that pizza and you can tell me all about it.'

I nodded and smiled. That's exactly what I did want. More than anything, I wanted someone unconnected with the whole situation to just sit down with and talk it over. Plus I never say no to pizza.

'Your bathroom is just through there,' she said. 'There are clean towels, soaps, shampoo, conditioner, tweezers and so on, everything you might need. Take your time, pamper yourself and I'll see you down in the kitchen when you're ready.'

Now a quick mention of the numerous emails I got about my advice to poor old Frustrated (with the boob-crushing boyfriend) a few days ago. Apparently I've now offended the entire male half of my readership as well as the Girl-Power brigade. So that's approximately eighty per cent of my readership I've managed to alienate in the last fortnight.

Just as well I'm not dependent on advertising revenue.

So a half-apology may be in order. I say half, because I feel my remarks were somewhat taken out of context. When I said all boys were animals I didn't mean it in a bad way – don't be so sensitive.

OK, now we've got that out of the way, can I get back to my blog? Sheesh!

Now, let's talk about your fears and phobias. Personally I'm terrified of clowns. God knows why. Maybe it has something to do with that time I was attacked by a gang of clowns in Milton Keynes. They tried to abduct me in their car but I managed to escape when the doors and wheels all came off. They gave chase but they kept tripping over their enormous clown feet. It was a truly horrible experience which has most probably scarred me for life. I'm not fond of Milton Keynes either, so that lends weight to the theory. Anyways, email and tell me what terrifies the bejaysus out of *you*.

Just got out the bath. Don't worry, I'm decent. Just wanted to say however much I love this bedroom, I love the bathroom more. Cheryl was right; there was everything I could need, including condoms! Is she trying to send me a message here? Like, 'Here in Futurehouse we believe in free love. Sex is fine as long as you're safe and happy . . .'

And I thought Mum was the hippy.

I am slightly paranoid now about the fact that Cheryl made sure to mention there was soap and tweezers in the bathroom. Is she saying I'm smelly and hairy? I made sure I scrubbed and plucked extra hard tonight. There's a phone in here. And a telly! I lay, soaking in a bubble bath, watching an old episode of *Friends* and tried calling Jugs. Still no answer. I tried Crumpet.

'Hello?'

'Hi Crumps, it's me. You down at the Fox tonight?'

'Hi babe, yes I suppose so, probably head down after dinner. Are you in Clifton?'

'Yep. Is Jugs gonna be there?'

'Dunno, she was a bit quiet at school. She'll probably be there.'

'OK, probably see you later then.'

'Yeah, seeya.'

I hung up and thought it over. Jugs might be there, but then again she might not. She didn't seem to want to talk to me. Maybe just rocking up wasn't the best idea. On the other hand, Poop-chute, who had said he wanted to see me, would definitely be at the Bull.

And so would The Boy.

I had one other thing to do. I called home.

'Hi Mum, I'm at Dad's, I'll be back on Sunday.'

Well, there was no easy way to say it.

She was silent for ages.

'Mum?'

'You must make your own choices,' she said, sounding a lot calmer than I'd expected.

'At least I'm phoning you,' I said, realizing as I said it that it sounded weak and defensive.

'Your brother and I have just come back from the DVD place,' she said quietly. 'He wanted a thing about superheroes, but I convinced him we should get something you might like.'

I rolled my eyes. Here we go with the guilt trip.

'Mum, I'm sorry I shouted at you, and I know you're angry at me for going when you told me not to, but this is important to me so I'm not going to apologize for my decision. I'll see you on Sunday and we can talk about it then if you like.'

She laughed a little scoffing laugh. 'Talking you can do, my girl. There's no doubt about that, but listening's another matter. Have a nice time.' And she hung up.

I felt a little sick just after that, but I put it out of my mind and got on with enjoying my bath. Mum spent half her life being mad at me even when I was being the perfect daughter, at least now I was actually doing something to earn the inevitable disapproval.

I came down nearly an hour after Cheryl had left me, pink and shiny, smelling of lavender and some Chanel *Allure* I'd found. Cheryl had laid the table with white plates and enormous wine glasses. 'White or red?' she asked.

Pre-loading in style.

Cheryl was a great listener; she never interrupted, just kept topping up my glass and handing me more chunks of garlic bread.

'I love this bread,' I said. 'Soft in the middle and crusty-sharp on the outside. Like me.'

'You see yourself as crusty?' she asked.

'Everyone sees me as crusty. I'm supposed to be the tough one. The one who's always there, being sane and normal. The one everyone tells their problems to.'

'You're the rock.'

'Well that makes me sound like Paul Burrell,' I said. 'I like to see myself as the lynchpin of the group.'

'Like Cheryl Cole?'

'Er, yes, I suppose.'

'And now you're living in Allerton, you feel isolated,' she said, nodding.

I sighed. 'Yeah, like my role's been taken away from me, and now the group's coming to pieces.'

'What does your mother say about it?' she asked before popping the tiniest piece of pizza into her mouth. She hadn't eaten much, I could see, whereas I'd scoffed more than half the pizza and most of the garlic bread already.

I shrugged. 'She doesn't really understand about friends. She thinks I should just make new ones in Allerton.'

Cheryl shook her head. 'It's not that easy. Friends are important.'

'I knew you'd understand,' I said.

Why did I say that? I hadn't known she would understand at all. It was just the wine.

I went to the Bull, trying not to think too hard about my reasons for doing so.

'Give me a call when you want me to come and get you,' Cheryl said as I got out.

'Are you sure?' I said. 'It's not too far to walk.'

'Don't walk!' she said. 'Please promise me you'll call me.'

'OK,' I said, smiling. 'Thanks Cheryl.'

'No problem,' she said and roared off up the street, narrowly missing a DHL van.

Poop was there of course, propping up the bar and talking to Jen, the barmaid. I snuck up behind him and put my hands over his eyes. 'Guess who?' I said.

'Hmmm, who do I know with fat fingers?' he said.

'Hey!' I protested. He turned and gave me a giant hug, squeezing harder than Fern Britton's gastric belt. 'I'm glad you're here,' he said.

I've known Poop for nearly ten years. Our mums are pals from way back. He's always been in the year above me and turned eighteen recently. We've had rows over the years and there have been times when we haven't spoken much to each other, but we've always been friends. And when Jugs told me she'd snogged Poop at Rory O'Byrne's summer party two years ago, I was so happy for them.

'How are you feeling?' I asked.

'Well my ankle's still swollen from rugby. And I've got a permanent cold. What about you?'

'My back's flared up again and I think I have meningitis.'

He sucked air through his teeth, then snapped his fingers.

'I've got cash!' he said. 'Fancy something sophisticated?'

'Really?'

'Yes, beer for you milady, and in a *bottle*.'

The good thing about the Bull was that the landlord turned a blind eye if you were underage as long as you stayed at the back and looked like you were drinking Coke. As long as the person buying the drinks was over eighteen (i.e. Poops or The Boy) he'd just leave us alone.

Jake and his friend Si turned up soon after, we crowded

into a snug and drank a toast. It felt good to be back. Poops was telling us about the fancy dress disco he, Jake and The Boy had been to on Saturday. Crumpet had told me she'd heard they might have had something to do with the smashing of Boots' windowpane.

The Boy went as a postbox. He couldn't get his arms out and had to talk through the letterbox all night. Jake went as Captain Jack Sparrow and Poops went as Fifi the Flowertot.

'Why?' I asked.

'Because they'd run out of Tweenies outfits.'

'Why did you want to be a Tweenie though?'

'I just like the big feet. Clomping about and that.'

'You are so random.'

'Not that I could have danced much, what with my ankle.'

'So what happened?'

'It was a bit flat, to be honest, so we left early and decided to go to Jake's place. We walked down the high street.'

'Still in your costumes?'

'Yes, The Boy was hilarious, little legs sticking out the bottom, tottering down the street. Anyway, we stopped outside Boots so he could light a cigarette.'

'Again, inside the postbox costume?'

'Yes, he kept blowing smoke rings out through the

letterbox. While we were waiting, Jake was practising his cutlass technique and overbalanced, falling into The Boy, who couldn't stay upright of course. So The Boy falls over against the windowpane and we hear it crack.'

Jake took over at this point. 'Then I saw a police car coming. I shouted, "Coppers, leg it!" I ran. Poops stopped to help The Boy get up and as he did, the entire window fell in.'

'I got him up,' Poops said. 'And we pegged it. Brave Pirate Jake was already halfway up Banbury St.'

'Only two types of pirates,' Jake said. 'The quick and the banged up.'

'The coppers stopped the car,' Poops said, 'and one got out to chase us. I couldn't run too fast with these bloody great feet, but I was a lot faster than The Boy. I turned to look and saw the copper crash-tackle him. The other copper had gone past in his car and was chasing Dwain Chambers here. So I stopped to watch, and I'm glad I did cos it was bare jokes. The copper wants to find The Boy's face so he has to roll him over and look for the letterbox, when he finds it he sort of peers in, looking for whoever's inside. Then he sees The Boy and points a finger at him. "Right," he says, "you're nicked."'

I couldn't help but laugh, but Poops shushes me. 'Wait,' he said, 'that's not the best bit. I heard The Boy from inside the postbox saying in this John Major voice,

"I have to inform you it is an offence to tamper with Royal Mail property." '

Well we all fell about at that point.

'Did he spend the night in jail?' Si asked when we'd stopped laughing.

'He certainly did,' Poops said. 'The Running Man and I both got away.'

Jake lifted his pint in triumph. 'The Boy has a court appearance next week,' he said.

Oh, Boy. What am I going to do about you?

And I don't remember much after that except sitting at a table with Poop and Jake and their mate Si and some bloke called Jeff who I'd never met, and drinking and roaring with laughter and The Boy turning up for last orders, he didn't say where he'd been. I don't remember what I said to him or how I ended up sitting on his knee and I definitely don't remember why I decided to pop out to the freezing beer garden with him when he went for a quick smoke, or how exactly we ended up snogging for so long that his cigarette sat in the ashtray and burned down all the way to the butt. I do distinctly remember The Boy saying he'd call me next week, he mentioned something about taking me to see a band.

Nor do I really remember phoning Cheryl, or her coming to pick me up, or Poop flirting with her outside the pub and making her giggle like a schoolgirl. I don't remember that on the ride home I gushed like one of Thames Water's leaky pipes and told her how great I thought she was.

I certainly don't remember saying that I wanted to come and live with her and Dad.

But I think I might have done.

Miss Understanding Blog Entry
– 27th February 2010

OK. I hardly drink alcohol for weeks and pay for it by getting drunk on two halves of lager. I feel just a little groggy this morning. At least I don't have to put up with Marley charging into my bedroom at 6.30 am and leaping on top of me with his damn claws. Though having said that, it would be nice to have someone warm to cuddle. He can be quite affectionate at times. And if you bribe him with comics he'll occasionally get you a cup of tea and bring it to you in bed.

I'm writing this in my massive bed at Cheryl's. (Hmmm, funny that I think of it as Cheryl's and not Dad's.) I didn't see the great man when I came in last night. It's probably just as well cos I was singing 'My Milkshake Brings *The Boy* to the Yard . . .' I guess he probably heard me. Ooh, knock on the door.

It was Cheryl, bringing me tea and toast. Did I mention

I love Cheryl?

'Did I say anything really embarrassing last night?' I asked, cringing.

'Not really, just after you got in the car you talked a lot about someone called The Boy.'

'OhmygodIdidnot!'

'Yes, then you started humming the Wedding March, *dah-da-da-dah*.'

'What! Did I?'

'No, not really. Did you see Jugs?'

'Um, no, she wasn't there.'

'She was at the Fox?'

'I guess so. I texted her a few times but she didn't respond.'

'Oh well. She'll contact you when she's ready. At least you saw your other friends.'

Well I saw some of them. I'm supposed to be here on a mercy mission, bringing the two groups back together, not choosing sides and getting sloshed with one of them. Oh what now? Phone call . . .

Oh *bollocks*!

OK. I've screwed it all up good and proper. The phone call was from Crumpet.

'Where were you?' she says.

'I went to the Bull. I hadn't heard from Jugs so I wasn't

sure if she wanted to see me. So I went to see Poops.'

'Oh right, because Jugs was big-time upset last night that you hadn't contacted her.'

'What? I sent her like a hundred texts!'

There was a pause.

'Do you have her new number?' she said.

There was another pause.

'She has a new number?' I said.

'Yes, she does.'

'Aww crap, no one told me.'

'I'm pretty sure you were copied in on the email,' Crumpet said. 'She had to change her number and email address when her mum's ex started stalking her.'

I was already trawling through my emails from Jugs. Sure enough there it was, unread. It had been filed in miscellaneous as it was from an unfamiliar address.

'I get hundreds of emails! Why didn't she text it to me?'

'I don't know. Don't worry, call her now, she'll understand.'

So I phoned straight away on her new number.

'Oh hello,' she sniffed.

'I'm so sorry babe, I was texting your old number. I thought you didn't want to see me.'

'I hear you were at the Bull last night,' she said.

Oh dear. 'Well yeah, I hadn't heard from you so I thought I'd better go and see Poops, he's really upset.'

'Not so upset you couldn't take a half-hour away from him in the beer garden snogging The Boy and inviting him to put his hand up your top.'

'He didn't put his hand up my top!'

'That's not what I heard; I heard it was like he was looking for lumps.'

Did I let him do that? I must have been *really* drunk.

'So Poops wasn't that upset then?' she repeated.

'Erm . . . Well he wasn't in tears, but—'

'It's fine, babe,' she interrupted. 'You made your choice.'

Now that wasn't fair.

'You sound like my mum,' I said.

'Well sorry I'm not so much fun as the boys. I was just over at the Fox crying my eyes out that my boyfriend of two years had dumped me for a fake blonde, and that my former best friend had come all the way over from bloody Allerton and hadn't even bothered to come and say hello.'

'I thought you didn't want to speak to me. You could have called, you know!'

'I *did*! You didn't answer.'

It took me a moment but then it clicked.

'Oh God, yes. Look I get a lot of calls from weirdos diverted from my website; I ignore the numbers I don't know. You changed your number; I didn't punch it into my phone, so my phone thought you were a stranger.'

'Yeah well now I think you're the stranger,' she snapped and hung up.

Bollocks again. What do I do now? Run a big bath and watch BBC Switch I suppose. Gotta sort my life out, but not when hung-over. I'm too tired to write more today. Sorry I haven't done the advice thing for a while, I'm not sure I have the bandwidth to deal with your emails today.

I'll sort your lives out for you soon though, Blogpals, don't worry.

PS No call from The Boy. I will *not* text him.

Later on 27th February 2010:

I feel a bit better, I had a bacon sarnie. I have missed bacon so much.

Thanks for all the emails telling me what scares you. By God you're a bunch of pansies aren't you? I'm surprised any of you ever has the courage to haul their quivering ass out the door and down to school of a morning.

Blingrrrl emailed to say she's frightened of jelly and pigeons. I'm assuming separately, like, she's scared of jelly, and she's also scared of pigeons. She's not just scared of, say, pigeons encased in jelly. That would be really terrifying.

Fat Gareth is apparently scared of being buried alive and suffocating, which, apparently was also the reason his last girlfriend gave for not wanting to sleep with him. Hahahahahahaplonk.

Jenna Hall says she lies in bed at night, tossing and turning in sweaty sheets, worrying about global warming. Hey, Jenna, open a goddamn window!

Daz Hall is scared witless by spiders, snakes and Craig David. I know! I thought it sounded strange too, but apparently a lot of spiders and snakes are poisonous, so it's not as irrational as it seems.

Two quite similar problems here, and you'll notice I come up with quite similar solutions, I'm nothing if not consistent.

Dear Miss Understanding

My belly-button piercing has become infected, I did it myself in RE with the blade off a pencil sharpener. I forgot to put Dettol on.

I didn't want to go to the doctor cos my mum cleans the surgery and she'd probably find out. So I used some of her peroxide cleaning fluid to kill the germs and mother XXXXXX (expletive deleted) I don't recommend you do that cos it hurt even more than the time I kicked a chisel and cut my big toe in half (video up on YouTube – search for toejamfootball).

Any thoughts?

Jackass

Hi Jackass

You're an idiot. Or to put it another way:

Hi Idiot

You're a Jackass. Suggest you go to your mum and say, Hey Mum, remember that time I kicked a chisel? Well I've done something that's not quite as stupid as that. I'm moving in the right direction at last. Baby steps, y'know.

After that, you're on your own.

Luv

Miss Understanding

Dear Miss Understanding

I'm seventeen, male, straight.

I woke up this morning with a pain in my gut. I thought I'd had a dodgy kebab but when I went to have a shower I saw I have a tattoo! I have no idea where it came from. I can't even really tell what it is. It looks like a marmoset trying to do a poo into my belly button.

I phoned my mate Dazzler cos I know he was out with me last night and he just fell about laughing, so I think I might have to go and kill him.

What am I going to do? How can I keep this secret from my mum? Help!

Thingie

PS I also have a steaming hangover, so any tips on that would be welcome too.

Dear Thingie,

OK, you're obviously feeling angry at yourself and worried sick about what your mum will say, so I won't rub it in, you numbskull.

The first thing that I thought of, was that you should go out and get plastered again and hope that when you wake up the tattoo will be gone just as magically as it appeared. Or at least will be a slightly better rendition of a defecating simian. But that's probably not going to work, nor will it get rid of your hangover.

Next I tried to think of ways you could hide it from your mum for the next year or so until you go off into the big, bad world. I thought maybe you could get really fat (if you're not fat already) and refuse to ever take off your top in front of her because you 'hate your body'.

But that's cutting off your nose to spite your face.

Then I wondered if you *should* cut off your nose to spite your face? No one would care about your tattoo if you were walking around with a great bleeding hole in your moosh. But I discounted it because it's just stupid.

And then I finally thought of the perfect solution.

Take a big glass, crack an egg into it. Add fruit juice, tomato juice and a slug of vodka. Drink it all and go back to bed. When you wake up go and tell your mum about the tattoo. Hey, don't complain. I fixed the hangover half

of your problem. Get your mum to sort out the other bit.
Who'dya think I am, Supernanny?

Love ya

Miss Understanding

Dear Miss U

I have quite a strange problem. I'm going out with this boy
from Newcastle. He's great, I really like him. He's well-fit and
a right laugh. Only problem is, I can't understand him most
of the time. It's all 'gan' this and 'howay the lads' that. I just
smile and nod most of the time.

The other night though, I think he wanted to have a
serious talk with me about our relationship and he sat me
down and went on in his silly accent for ages and then said
whayyaken? And I didn't know what to say. I asked for some
time to think it over and he agreed.

Since then he hasn't called me. What's happened? Have
we split up? Are we having some space? Is he waiting for me
to tell him I'll marry him? What do I do?

Love

Trina

Hey Trina

That's a *good* one. That really had me stumped for a while.
I had to go and stand on my head before I could come up
with the solution. I had a similar experience myself you

know, on holiday in Greece last year. Stefanos didn't speak a word of English, and I only knew enough Greek to order simple food.

That proved to be more than enough to fuel our romance. We'd walk along a moonlit beach, the waves lapping at our feet. He'd stop me, swing me about and mouth some meaningless gobbledook. I'd clutch his muscular arms, look deep into his bright eyes and reply in perfect Greek: 'Twelve kleftakos and a bottle of retsina please.'

Anyway, enough about me, here's what you should do. Text him and arrange to meet. Sit him down and don't let him talk. Say something like: 'You've had your say, and I've been thinking things over. Now it's your turn to listen to me.' Then make up some crap about him being your rock, or your lucky star, or the love of your life. The thing is it doesn't really matter. You don't have to answer his exact question. Just say what it is *you* want to say. Like a politician.

He's not going to sit there, listen to you pour your heart and then turn around and say, 'Yes, but I'm afraid I must press you for your response to the question I asked last week.'

If he does push it, just say, 'Never mind about that now, the important thing is that I love/respect/appreciate/dislike you, isn't that enough?'

Yours

Miss 'Babel' Understanding

Still no contact from The Boy.

Back home again. Dinner with Dad and Chezza went well last night. Dad was a little quiet. He's trying to figure out the solution to some complex engineering problem and has his head even further into the clouds than usual. He hardly ate anything either, just kept building ramparts with his peas.

That was OK, Cheryl provides more than enough entertainment. She's one of those people who assumes everyone knows everyone. 'You know Ged, don't you?' she started.

'No,' Dad said.

'Yes you do, Ged was going out with Mara, until Mara went lesbian again. He has the double-jointed knees.'

Dad looked puzzled.

'You'd think you'd remember that, Dad,' I said.

'You *do* remember,' Cheryl continued. 'He moved to the new estate other side of Barrington and started going out with that girl who has the pig's heart.'

'I really don't think I know *her*, either,' he said, frowning.

'You must know her, she ran the crystal shop in Lower Allerton, she's best friends with Greta.'

'And Greta is . . . ?'

'Greta? You know Greta; she did the Great Northern Run dressed as a kettle. She blew her whistle so much she collapsed at the eighth mile and was on the telly drinking lucozade in a silver blanket.'

And so on.

I liked it. I felt at home there. And I know it's awful to say, but I'm glad it wasn't just me and my dad. I really don't know what to say to him.

Anyway, I feel I've bored you too much with tales of my tedious life. I'll just fill you in on what happened when I got back here this morning. The conversation with Mum went something like this.

'Oh. Run out of clean knickers?' She was tidying. Which to her means moving stuff about until she finds something interesting enough to distract her.

'Actually I was worried you might get in trouble with the Scientologists if you missed your class tonight,' I said, putting on the kettle. 'I didn't want Marley frightened by the giant mother ship come to take you away to planet Zorg for re-education.'

'Don't speak to me like that,' she said, eyes narrowing. 'You're in enough trouble as it is.'

'Oh leave it out,' I said. 'You're just cranky because for once you had to miss your precious Bikerack yoga.'

'It's Bikram yoga,' she huffed. 'I don't do that one any

more on account of my foot. It was Reiki on Saturday morning.' She picked up a pile of *Sunday Times* colour supplements and moved them to another chair. 'For your information, Missy, I didn't miss my session.'

'What? Well who looked after Marley? You didn't leave him on his own?'

'No of course not, Lance looked after him.'

'Because if you . . . hold on, who's Lance?'

'Lance is a man I know, he's a plumber.'

'You can't leave Marley alone with your plumber!' I sputtered.

'He's not just *a* plumber; I've known him for ages.'

'It's just not right . . . hang on. What do you mean you've known him for ages? In what capacity?'

'As a plumber and a . . . and as a friend.'

'A friend?' I said, peering at her intently. 'You mean *boy*friend?'

'Don't leap to conclusions, darling. I'm allowed to have friends, aren't I?'

'Of course, but don't you think you should let me know when one of these "friends" is in sole care of my brother?'

'If you'd answered your phone I would have done so,' she countered, checkmating me neatly.

I screamed and ran up to my room. As soon as I walked in I realized she'd been in there, nosing about. She hadn't even tried to hide it, leaving drawers open and the bedspread pulled back. I ran to the top of the stairs.

'I took the condoms and drugs with me,' I yelled. 'That's why you couldn't find them when you searched my room.'

'Don't be a child,' she yelled back.

I lay on my bed trying to calm down. But then I heard her come creaking up the stairs. She opened the door.

'I don't like being an angry-shouty mother,' she said quietly. 'I like being a calm, reasonable mother.'

I said nothing, watching her.

'But I can adapt,' she went on. 'If you are prepared to act like a grown-up, like an equal, with an equal share of responsibilities, then I can be myself. If you choose to act like a child, then I can be a vicious hell-beast. It's up to you.'

'I'm not here to enable your character flaws, Mum,' I replied. 'Maybe it's you that needs to grow up. Maybe I don't want you to be yourself. Maybe I want you to be a proper mother.'

I could see that I'd hurt her, but she didn't reply. She just walked out and slammed the door.

Later I think I heard her crying in bed.

Dear Miss Understanding

My boyf and I have been having sex for ages (I mean lots of

different sex at different times not one big long lot of sex all at once just now) and we've been really careful and safe but a couple of weeks ago I missed my period and I had a test but it was a false alarm which was cool but before I found out there was no baby my boyf went all postal on me and said I must be having it off with someone else because we'd only ever done it with a condom so I asked my friend and she said that condoms are only ninety-seven per cent defective which means if you do it one hundred times you'll have three babies and me and my boyf must have done it nearly one hundred times if you count the ones when things happened a bit too quick for him to really need a condom if you know what I mean so that was a lucky escape but how do you find out these things cos I don't remember this from sex ed.

Help!!!

LaGwen

Dear Gwen

Before I answer your question I have a little housekeeping to do. Having it off? Boyf? Multiple exclamation marks? No, no, no. This isn't good enough. You're not ready for sex, Gwen. You need to learn to read and write first. I know this sounds harsh, but if I don't tell you this no one else will. It's *not* OK to be ignorant; it's *not* OK to be lazy. Not when you're nine months away from having to squeeze a ten-pound poo machine out through your lady garden.

You think reading the warning on a pack of condoms is too hard? Try filling out an application for Child Tax Credit.

You ask how you find out about the risk level of using condoms? Hmmm, that's a tough one. If only there were some gigantic global database of information accessible through a computer where you could look for this kind of information. I don't know, some kind of web, or net, or something.

But I guess there isn't anything like that is there? I guess it's all a little too hard isn't it? Just like grammar is too hard, and punctuation, and probability, and keeping your pants on.

Yours in love-more-than-anger

Miss Understanding

Dear Miss Understanding

I'm Sally, the girl you told to stop seeing the ex-prisoner. I tried to break up with him but he cried and it nearly broke my heart. He asked for another chance and said he'd been really hopeful about his future now I am in it. I told him I'd think it over. He was in prison for fraud. Writing bad cheques. He's no pervert or thug or anything. I really don't want to break up with him, what do you think?

Hopefully yours

Sally

Well, well, maybe I was wrong for once. Never let it be said I don't own up to my mistakes, even if this one was really your fault for not telling me what he was banged up for in the first place.

I hereby change my advice; I think you should see the guy and have lots of babies together.

Good luck.

Miss U

Still haven't had an email from Al (or The Boy, but I've given up hope there). I can't say I'm surprised about Al really. I didn't really believe him when he said he wasn't going to read my blog. And flicking back over the last few entries, I see that he might not have appreciated me talking about what happened on our date. And also some references to a certain Boy that may have crept in from time to time. Look, I can't be for ever censoring myself just to avoid offending people, can I? This is me, warts and all.

PS I don't have warts. That was just an expression.

Miss Understanding Blog Entry
– 4th March 2010

Sigh. I saw Al at school yesterday, and I think he blanked me. If you're reading this Al, I'm sorry. Any chance we could just be friends?

Home Front: 'Lance says we shouldn't reheat rice on the Aga,' Marley informed me yesterday. I could sense Mum stiffen at the sound of the name. She was sitting at the kitchen table knitting a hemp jumper that I was really hoping wasn't my birthday present.

'In Versailles, during the court of Louis XIV,' I told him, 'etiquette dictated that nobles weren't allowed to pay any attention to people who hadn't been formally introduced to them.'

'Eddy Cat?' Marley said, looking perplexed.

'I mean unless someone introduced you to someone else, you had to pretend they weren't there and that you couldn't hear what they were saying.'

'But that's stupid, why couldn't they just introduce themselves?'

'Because that would let the person who was *supposed* to be introducing them, off the hook,' I said, loudly. 'Their obvious and awkward refusal to acknowledge one another would be a source of extreme embarrassment to *that* person who really should have known better.'

'So what does that have to do with Lance?' he asked.

I sighed.

'Nothing really. Never mind. But I've been reheating chicken tikka biryani on this Aga for you since you were three and you're fine, aren't you?'

'Apart from the diabetes,' he said, clutching his tummy.

'Yes, of course,' I said. 'Apart from the diabetes.'

Blue Sky Corner: Thanks for the responses to my request for your God-awful first dates.

The worst were as follows:

Hellgirl wrote in to tell me an ex-boyfriend took her joyriding on their first date, with three of his mates in the back of a Renault Clio. The police called out the chopper and they ended up abandoning it in the retail park and hiding in the trash compactor behind Pets at Home. Just as well you don't have to dry-clean polyester. What I find most worrying about Hellgirl's description is that she makes it clear that this was the first, but by no means the last date she had with this guy. What was the second date? Ram-raiding Argos?

Still, I'd prefer that to Willow Thomas's first date with the boy who is now her ex. She'd made the mistake of feigning a vague interest in role-playing games so he got his dad to take the two of them on a three-hour round-trip to the Dungeons and Dragons Convention at the NEC. She says, 'The day was saved though by my realization that I was by far the most attractive female within a mile of the place. I could have put on a barbarian queen's outfit and had four hundred spod slaves worshipping me.'

Jenna Hall writes in with just three words: curry and kickboxing. (What, together, Jenna?)

Ben Noakes was seduced by a sturdy, outdoorsy lass he met on holiday in Yorkshire. Then, she took the poor sod fell walking. Ben had visions of a gentle country stroll with maybe a picnic and a quick snog on a blanket. But no. 'I understand now why they call it fell walking,' he says. 'I fell so many times it would have been quicker for me to just stay down and crawl. She did try to snog me at the end but she had dried sheep dung stuck in her hair so I gave it a swerve.'

And this week's winner is Georgia Banks. 'This boy I knew asked me out and he took me to the library. "WTF?"

I said. "Who goes on a date to the library? That's mental."
He said it was a "study date" and after we'd finished our
Eng Lit essays we could read some poems to each other.
What a loser.'

I dunno Georgia, it could have been worse, he could
have taken you to an abandoned warehouse and
handcuffed you to a radiator. And *then* read you poems.

Email from <u>Anya.Buxton@notmail.com</u>
To: J_Buxton@clayjones.co.uk
OK Dad, I'm not going to beat around the bush. This is
awkward and I want you to give me an honest answer.
Can I come and live with you? Mum is doing my head in.
I've been getting further reports from Marley about this
weirdo who keeps floating around the house. His name's
Lance, he's a plumber and even worse, apparently he's a
keen rambler. I've never met the bloke but I've seen
evidence of his existence. He keeps leaving boiled eggs
and Ordnance Survey maps around the place. Nuff said.
I haven't met him yet, and frankly, I don't want to.

I know what you're going to say, that it's too far to go
to school every day, but I can take the early bus and study
on the way – I've got my laptop (thanks again for that).
Loads of students come in from further away and if it all
proves too much, I can always transfer back to Clifton.
Don't worry about the 'upheaval', Clifton's a better school

and you know me, I'll ace my A-levels wherever I am.

I also know that you offered once before to let me live with you and I think I told you to go and stick your head in a bucket of sick, but I was much younger then and didn't appreciate just how annoying Mum could be in a rarefied atmosphere.

Lots of love

An

Miss Understanding Blog Entry
– 5th March 2010

Received this email today:

Dear Anya

We'd *love* to have you stay with us. I talked it over with your father last night. Don't worry about the journey to Allerton, I have to go most mornings anyway for one thing or another, so would be happy to take you. And, as you say, there's always the bus should I be busy with something else.

Your father is going to phone your mother tomorrow, so perhaps you'd like to confirm with her first – I presume you've already broached the subject? I really think you need to talk to her if you haven't already.

What we'd suggest is that you come to stay with us for a month to begin with as a sort of 'trial period'. If it all works out we can make it a permanent arrangement and we can talk about schools.

I'm so excited. I know this isn't about me, but I'm really looking forward to having you come and stay with us, and am sure this is the best solution for all concerned.

Much love

Cheryl

Hmmm.

Don't get me wrong, this is the result I'm looking for and I'm over the moon, but a few things bother me about this email. One – why isn't Dad writing it? Who wears the pants over there? Two – having said that, the 'trial period' bit sounds like something my dad would come up with. It's hardly the news a loving daughter wants to hear. Three – Cheryl's just about edging into hysteria in her excitement about me coming. It's all a bit Hansel and Gretel if you ask me. I can tell you for nothing Chezza, I'm going to slam doors, drop pizza on the sofa and stomp about saying, 'It's not fair'.

Oh wells. No point looking a gift horse in the mouth. I can smell the Sanctuary bath scrub already.

Blue Sky Corner: I went to see the Career Guidance Counsellor on Tuesday. Anyone else had that pleasure? If so, email me in what she suggested *you* should be, and what you want to be. The grossest mismatch wins a prize. I'll kick things off. She said, almost before I'd sat down,

'What do you want to do when you leave school?'

Hold on, I thought. Why not have a little chat first before barging into the personal questions? We're not speed-dating.

I said, 'I'm going to be a writer.'

'Do you have a plan B?' she said even before I'd finished saying the '. . . ter' bit of writer.

'Of course,' I replied. 'If I can't be a writer, I want to be a talk-show host.'

'Hmmm,' she said, trying to hide the look of despair on her face. She looked at my file. 'Your results in English are quite good. What about secretarial?'

Who is this woman?

'Fine,' I agreed. 'Put me down for that.'

'Great,' she said.

'Or astronaut. Put down astronaut too,' I said. 'Just in case.'

Dear Miss Understanding

Hi it's me, Barrelgirl. You asked for more information about Josh, well I wasn't sure you'd want to know too much about what happens in the bedroom, but let's just say he's extremely athletic. Think David Beckham with a man's voice. He also knows his way around a woman's body. Max can't even *find* my body once he's taken his contacts out.

Max is really quite old; we went shopping together the

other day, we both wanted a black suit. Me because black hides bulges very well. He because he has a school-friend's funeral to go to next week.

So what do you think?

Barrelgirl

Dear Barrelgirl,

You weren't sure I'd want to know what happens in the bedroom? Have you actually been reading my blog? Finding out what goes on in other people's bedrooms is what gets me up in the morning.

I was plumping for Max after your first email, now I'm on Josh's team. Oh I'm as confused as you. Tell you what. Why don't you go out on one more date with each of them, tell me all about it and then we'll decide together, does that sound OK? While you're on this date, I want you to look each of them in the eyes and think to yourself – could I live with this bloke staring back at me across the kitchen table, boiled egg on his chin, for the rest of my life?

That's all for now, bye, love you bye.

Miss Understanding less and less of this crazy world every day

Dear Anya
Please, please, please, don't put this on your blog. If you do

I'll never speak to you again and I'll start a rumour that you're a really bad kisser. (You're not.)

I just wanted to say that I don't hate you, I understand why you wrote about our date. That's just who you are, you're a writer and you feel you need to share everything; fair enough, just leave me out, OK? I'm not like that, and if you want me to be a friend, you have to accept *my* terms.

I would like to be your friend, and I would like to keep emailing you, but only if it's off-the-record, as it were.

Deal? Or No Deal?

Al

Miss Understanding Blog Entry
– 8th March 2010

Oh my God! That woman! There's nothing, NOTHING that's OK about her. All I can say is, Jocasta couldn't be a more fitting name. For those of you who don't read, Jocasta is a fictional character from a Greek myth. She was Oedipus's mother. You remember Oedipus, that old motherf*****r? How's poor Marley supposed to deal with that? He's going to go to school one day, read *Oedipus Rex* and Mum tucking him into bed will never be the same again.

Speaking of history, we all have to write an essay this week on 'Warfare in Roman Times'. Dan Boyle told me he was intending to play World of Warcraft for a couple of hours and just write down everything that happens. 'Did they have Orcish Zeppelins in Roman times?' I asked. He wasn't sure.

Personally I'm just going to cut-and-paste from Wiki. I

get around the whole plagiarism thing by translating the text into Italian in Babelfish, then translating it back and running a spelling and grammar check. It comes out perfectly well in a grammatical sense, but with enough errors of fact to not arouse suspicion.

It would be probably quicker to just write the stupid essay myself, but where's the fun in that? That's what they *want* you to do.

It's boring here. Dinner seemed to last for hours. Marley kept toying with his food, as usual. Mum looked over and clucked sympathetically. 'Next time maybe I should put fewer tomatoes in the quinoa, yes?' she asked him.

Marley looked panicked, but controlled himself. 'How about,' he said, 'next time you put fewer quinoa in the tomatoes?'

'Less quinoa,' I corrected.

Marley thought this over. 'Or how about, *no* quinoa?' he said hopefully.

'It's packed with vitamin D,' Mum protested.

'So are vitamin D tablets,' I pointed out. 'Crush one up and bung it into a plate of spaghetti hoops like a normal mother.'

'Just eat, both of you,' Mum said.

'Count yourself lucky,' I told Marley, 'I've got gluten-free quinoa.'

'We can all count ourselves lucky,' Mum said brightly. 'I went down to the farmer's market today and got us some acai berries for dessert.'

'Great,' said Marley and I, miserably.

Hey Al,
Deal.
  Anya

Miss Understanding Blog Entry
– 12th March 2010

Just what I needed to cheer me up. Lots of great responses to my request for career guidance mismatches.

Blake Grimshaw tells me: 'I wanted to be a Formula One driver (not so out-there as it might seem, my dad's a rally driver and I race go-karts most weekends) but she didn't even ask about that. According to my "profile" I'd make an excellent gardener. I'm allergic to bloody pollen!'

'She told me I should be a Community Awareness Officer,' writes Kayleigh Leach, 'whatever that is. I told her I wanted to be a lawyer, and she shuddered. She actually shuddered. Then she had a think and said, "Tour guide?"'

Hannah Goodluck says she shrugged and said, 'Dunno, shop assistant?' And the GC beamed, wrote it down and said, 'Works for me.'

Jared Freeman wants to be an engineer but apparently

he should work more on his fitness for when he joins the Army.

And when Kelly Binns said, 'Two-bit pole dancer,' without blinking the GC nodded and said, 'You're doing my job for me.'

OK, that last one's not true, but it so could be.

Miss Understanding Blog Entry – 15th March 2010

I left home yesterday.

Can I say that again? Skip it if you're bored.

I left home yesterday.

Dad came and collected me. Mum had taken Marley out for the morning by unspoken agreement after I'd told her Dad was coming to get me.

She didn't really say anything about my decision. To be fair to her, she had always said she wouldn't stand in my way should I make the decision to live with Dad, but I think she only said that because she was sure it would never happen. Mum can't understand how anyone could want to live with Dad, and even worse, how someone could want to live with someone who wanted to sleep in Dad's bed.

Marley was a bit upset when I told him. But I said he could come and visit me whenever he wanted and I'd talk to Dad about getting a laser installed in the roof. That cheered him up.

I love it here. I love my new life. I love living in an interior design magazine. I'm not Monica-from-*Friends* obsessive-compulsive you understand but it's actually making me want to tidy up after myself. It helps having a room-sized wardrobe of course. I've nearly filled it already, even though I don't remember bringing that much, and when I need to put more stuff in I have to slam the door shut quickly. It's a bit like a Tom and Jerry cartoon when Tom opens a cupboard and loads of junk falls out and buries him.

Not all mail I get from you bunch of saddoes is asking for advice, quite a lot of it is criticism of my blog specifically and me generally. That's fine. I can give as good as I get. But there have been a few emails lately telling me to stop going on so much about my family and friends. A lot of people seem to want to hear more about what's going on at school, or more likely in the car park behind Zeon on an early Sunday morning. Bonnie Greaves says, 'OK, thanks for all the information about your web-footed friends back in Incestville, but now you live in civilization maybe you could concentrate on Allerton a bit more?' Fat Gareth agrees but has fed his reply through a websaurus. 'Your columns, though engaging and amusing have lately possessed a quality of solipsism.'

Huh?

On the other hand I do get a significant amount of web-traffic expressing interest in my sad little life. Which is nice, if a little odd. 'You is jokes, man,' says Tooz. Jenna Hall asks, 'Can we have more about your mum?' and Mischa Henton-Brookes emailed to ask if I could post photos of the 'cast of characters' as if this is the world's most drawn-out play. 'The Boy sounds dreamy,' Bluegrass says innocently.

So I need a straw poll here. Please drop me a line and let me know whether you want less, same or more about my life. I'm nothing if not adaptable, as that bloke who gave birth to a baby said.

Dear Miss Understanding
I'm worried I might need to realign my self-image. I've always thought of myself as being OK-looking. I'm slim, and tall, but not too tall. I have good-sized boobs and a normal-looking face.

Problem is, all the buff blokes I like ignore me or just want to be friends, and I get this constant stream of munter-types asking me out. I'm too scared to put my face up on amihot.com. Any help?

Cheers,

Confused

Dear Confused

OK, firstly, even if you are mingier than Emperor Ming of Mingworld, don't worry about it. You'll find the right guy out there eventually. Think of all the crusties you see. Almost all of them have found someone, even the skulking rat-faced ones you see stubbing out their fags outside Morrisons.

I mean, someone even married Wayne Rooney!

Secondly, look on the bright side, it's theoretically possible you may not be a munter at all. By the sounds of it, you're just a friendly, self-aware girl with a positive self-image. You're also apparently very approachable. I bet the munters ask you out not because they see you as being on their rung of the looks-ladder, but because you smile sweetly at them when other girls don't. Boys try to take advantage of nice girls who they think may be willing to offer a sympathy-snog.

The buff blokes probably aren't interested for the same reason: they like bad girls, they like mean girls, they like girls who lead them on, then drop them flat, then start all over again, just because they can. Just like girls go for men who are bastards, boys go for girls who are bitches.

So regardless of whether you are good-looking or not, your approach should be the same, just carry on as you are, eventually you'll find the right guy.

Love

Miss Understanding

Dear Miss Understanding,

I know I'm going to sound stupid, but is it normal to have one boob bigger than the other? Ms Cooper was demonstrating in Science how much bigger the Earth is than the Moon by showing us models?

Well, those models looked like my tits.

Luv

Blingrrrl

Dear Blingrrrl

You're not stupid, you're just ignorant.

Yes, it is normal. Though if your boobs are in fact as large as the models I've heard Ms Cooper was showing then you could probably make a decent living as a different sort of model altogether.

By the way. Boys. Do. Not. Care. They'll be happy just to get a quick peek at one. Show them the moon-sized one first. Always leaving them wanting more.

Love

Miss Boob-tastic Understanding

Miss Understanding Blog Entry
– 19th March 2010

Wow, you guys are amazing! Thanks to everyone who emailed me to vote in the straw poll. I got over a hundred replies, not including the three asking me if I wanted Viagra (?) and the one from a Nigerian Prince dripping with blood diamonds asking me for my account details so he could propose to me or something (the details were sketchy).

And when I saw how many of you seemed to want me to carry on talking about my personal life I nearly cried, even though I know you're all just shaking your heads in amusement at what a fool I am and how awful my family is.

I don't mind being a figure of fun to you all, as long as you're *having* fun. If I'm going to be a writer one day, I have to get used to entertaining people with my personal revelations.

So Fat Gareth, Bonnie Greaves and all you others.

Sorry, you're going to have to put up with it, or go elsewhere for your vicarious amusement.

Obviously I will keep reporting on the doings of the more colourful members of staff at Woodyatt, and if Kelly Binns goes through with the beerboarding party she's rumoured to be having at half-term, I will definitely crash that and report back.

Someone asked me about how I came to move to Allerton in the first place. It's a long story and I don't want to go into that in too much detail but it involves my mum, my dad's week-old Audi TT and a lamp-post.

Dad moved out soon after that incident; he went to live in a new house he'd built and asked me and Marley to go and live with him. We were angry at him then (or I was) and told him to get lost, it was only later I began to suspect that Mum's accident was only the latest in a long string of rubbish things she'd done and I started to have some sympathy with him.

Mum wanted to move away from Clifton cos she didn't want to keep running into him, but she didn't want to go too far because of work, and Allerton has an OK school for me and a good school for Marley, so here we are. I don't mind because I can go back and forth when I like. I live here in Clifton officially. But if it were a hundred miles away from Marley I don't think I could do it.

* * *

That'll do for now, I don't want you to think I'm going overboard on the internal monologue.

Let's have some of your emails:

Dear Miss Understanding

My boyfriend is a total stoner and he's getting worse. He and his mates started experimenting with weed a few months ago. It was sort of funny at first and I even tried some myself, but it made me think I could see little musical notes come out of the stereo and float about the room when Lily Allen was on and then I was sick on my laptop. So I'm not touching the stuff any more. When I go to see him he just wants to sit about doing nothing but smoking spliffs, eating Doritos and watching TV. Multi-slacking, he calls it. He hardly ever seems to want to kiss me any more, and his breath makes me feel sick even when he does.

Also he talks in slow motion now. It's all, 'Duuude, baaby,' etc. I want to slap him. The thing is, I really like this guy. Don't ask me why, he's not that good-looking, he's got no money, his school results are awful and he works on the carvery at the Shovel Inn so always smells of overdone lamb. And weed, of course.

How do I A) stop my boyfriend from smoking so much dope, or B) stop liking him so much?

Rollergirl

* * *

151

Hey Rollergirl

Whoa, this is a toughie. Really I should be referring you to a drugs counsellor, or something. But you're no dummy, you know that option's available, right? I think the reason you're writing to me is that you think getting your boyfriend to go and see a professional is about as likely as Johnny Vegas winning the London Marathon.

So here's what I suggest. You've got to break him out of his lifestyle. I've done some research and apparently cannabis is addictive, but not nearly so much as heroin or nicotine. He's more addicted to the lifestyle of being a stoner than the drug itself. You need to show him how life can be so much better than that. But he'll need an incentive; tell him you want to go to Morocco, where the finest cannabis comes from. Explain to him in one-syllable words that you'll need money.

If you can get him excited enough about it, you can get him to stop spending all his money on rubbish local dope and save it up instead. Persuade him to do extra shifts at the Shovel Inn (though not on Thursdays because sometimes I go with my mates on a Thursday). The idea is to break the cycle, separate him from his friends, his dope and his habit. Once he's safely over the border then it's up to you to try and persuade him not to go back.

And obviously don't, whatever you do, actually go anywhere near Morocco. Change your mind at the last minute and take him to Switzerland instead, it's about as drug-friendly as the Amish Olympic Committee.

Yours

Miss 'Just-Say-No' Understanding

Cheryl is giving me driving lessons!

'I'm not seventeen for another five months,' I told her.

'You can apply for your provisional licence in two months,' she pointed out. 'It took me a year before I passed my test.'

Yeah, it's not going to take *me* that long, I thought. I like Cheryl and everything, but she is in fact the most dangerous driver there has ever been since that yappy one from *Speed Racer* drove off that cliff.

But I warmed up to the idea when I realised she'd be teaching me to drive in *her car*. The BMW. It has heated seats and everything. I made her show me how the iPod dock worked first of all. It's totally intuitive. I played Duffy at top volume (which is incredibly top in that machine) so as to drown out the sound of gear crunching. We drove all the way around the house in first gear and Cheryl opened the top so she could smoke a fag and we froze our tits off and just laughed and laughed. Talk about female bonding. Afterwards we both felt a bit awkward with each other like you do when you meet a new friend who you think you're really going to like and you take it all a bit too fast.

* * *

Dad was home quite early last night and we had dinner together. Cheryl said she'd had a call from my Uncle Henry that day and Dad should phone him back.

'Henry?' Dad said, smiling. 'What's the old fool up to these days?'

Now this is one of the problems with Dad. Why is he asking his new wife, who barely knows Henry, what his own brother is up to? Why doesn't he already know what Henry is up to? I know men are generally rubbish at this sort of thing, i.e. talking to each other, but Dad takes it to new levels. Unless you hold his head between your hands and speak slowly and clearly right into his face then he doesn't seem to pay attention to anything that's going on. He seems to only have enough room in his brain for one thing at a time. That's why his buildings are so cold and clinical I reckon. He likes clean surfaces, unbroken lines, simple shapes and empty spaces.

Cheryl is good for him, I tell myself as she fills him in on Henry's new business selling mobile phones to emerging Europe. It's a good idea, the first thing people want to do after emerging from the restraints of Tyrannical Communism is to start texting each other. Plenty of time to text your mates while you're in the bread queue.

'How's Jenny?' Dad asked. Jenny is Henry's wife.

'She's fine,' Cheryl said.

'No kids still?'

'No, I don't think she wants kids really. Such a shame,' she said, wistfully.

'Yes, Henry would make a great father,' Dad said.

'Really?' I piped up. 'Cos he makes a crap uncle.'

Dad looked at me in surprise.

I shrugged. 'I never see him.'

'His loss, darling,' Cheryl said, and started taking away the plates. I sat at the table with my father for a few moments; he looked uncomfortable, obviously trying to think of something to say. I rolled my eyes and got up to help Cheryl with the dishwasher.

'What are you going to do about your friends?' she asked.

'Dunno,' I replied. 'I need to try and get them together in the same place as Jugs now isn't talking to Poop *or* me.'

'What about a party?' she said. 'Make sure everyone who's anyone is there and she'll definitely turn up.'

'Even if she knows Poop's going to be there?'

'Especially if Poop's going to be there. She's a girl isn't she? She'll want to be there, looking fabulous, letting him know what he's missing. Even if she's so mad at him she wants to cut all his suits in half.'

'Poop doesn't have any suits, but I take your meaning,' I said. 'But where could we have this party?'

She shut the dishwasher, stood and looked at me,

shining like a hundred-watt, high-carbon light-bulb, looking about a billion times prettier than my mum and a hundred years younger.

'We can have it here,' she said.

Staff Watch: O happy day, praise be to the Lord of the mobile-phone camera, thanks muchly to the anonymous reader who sent me the snaps, taken in Zeon over the weekend showing a blurry, but eminently recognizable Ms Cooper chomping lips with our old friend Mr Graves the PE teacher. To post, or not to post? That is the question.

Oh you know the answer, against my better judgement, I've put the dirty pics up on the site here: CoopsandGraves@zeon/missunderstanding.net

But let's keep this between us, OK? No emailing the link to dozens of your friends, please . . .

Hey, tell me if this is weird. I found Cheryl opening Dad's post the other day. Is that allowed? I asked her about it and she said she opens all of his 'household' post. Whatever *that* means. Maybe my mum isn't so far off when she calls her the Housekeeper.

Hmmm, maybe all marrieds do that, though I'm sure Mum never took it upon herself to open Dad's post.

Maybe she should have?

Miss Understanding Blog Entry
– 10th April 2010

First an email from Barrelgirl, she of the two boyfriends.

Hey Miss Understanding

Well, I did what you said, I went out on a date with each of them. First Max. He took me to dinner at his health club. Very exclusive, lots of fake tan, fake teeth and fake tits. Half the women there were half the age of their husbands, the other half were the same age as their husbands but desperately trying to look half as young as the others to avoid their other half ditching them for a woman half his age. Hope that makes sense.

Either way, I fell into the first half. I've never seen such a lovely gym. Should be lovely, as no one ever uses the equipment, he told me, or the pool. They just sit in the bar and watch each other, trying to spot who's had what work done.

Anyway I had a really nice time. Max is very funny really, and I did as you said. I looked into his face over coffee and wondered if I could spend the rest of my life with him, or more realistically, could I spend the rest of *his* life with him.

Then two days later I went out with Josh. He took me to the Springflower Festival near Gloucester. He'd wanted to take a tent and stay over but I told him I had to be back. We had an amazing time, there were some great acts on and we danced up near the front, drank cider and ate a burger from a dodgy-looking concession. As we sat in the grass, just watching each other and smiling, munching on sweet beef and soft bread, cider bubbles dancing on my lips, I thought again about what you said and just then I made up my mind.

I'm not going to tell you who I decided to go with. I need to tell them both first, then I'll let you know, is that OK?

Thanks for your help Miss Understanding, you're unique, you know that?

Love

Barrelgirl

Dear Barrelgirl

Unique you say? Well they don't teach this stuff at evening classes you know.

Good luck with the difficult breaking-up conversation.

One tip though, make sure the guy you like isn't just about to dump you before you break-up with the other one.

Yours cynically,

MU

Dear Miss Understanding

My girlfriend won't shave. She's so hairy! We're not talking fine downy hairs either, these buggers are thick, black and wiry. She took her leggings off last night and it was like going to bed with King Kong.

She says shaving is 'a patriarchal dictate intended to de-humanize women'. Yeah, maybe, but yesterday the zipper on my fleece caught against her pit hairs and tore a matted chunk out. She said I did it on purpose but I swear it was an accident.

This is becoming a health and safety issue, what do I do?

Yours,

Grimble

Dear Grimble

Luckily I have some experience dealing with hippy-chicks. What I'd suggest is this: tell her you've discovered this new eco-business that collects human hair and turns it into blankets for the elderly so they can whack down their heating. Make up some old crap about human hair providing twenty-seven per cent more insulation per pound than sheep's wool.

Then hand her a razor, a biodegradable bin-liner and suggest to her you celebrate saving the planet afterwards by creating a little global warming of your own.

The only flaw I can see is that she might expect you to join in on the old depilation-frenzy. Small price to pay, you might think, but I've heard the back, sack and crack can sting a tad . . .

Riiiiiippppp!

Miss Understanding

Dear MU

My boyfriend Balthazar (please don't use his real name) went to Center Parcs with his parents over Christmas and was away for two weeks, I was really lonely and ended up snogging a boy against the fruit machine at the Fat Goose. I hardly even remember it but someone took a photo and it somehow got back to Balthazar. We talked it through and got over it, but then a couple of weeks ago I heard that he'd snogged Bonnie Greaves (please *do* use her real name) in the car park behind Tesco's.

Fat Gareth was there and says Balthazar wasn't even drunk as he'd only had one and a half glasses of shandy. When I confronted Balthazar about it, he said, 'Well now we're square,' and left it at that.

How am I supposed to respond?
Blingrrrl

Dear Blingrrrl

Well, well, what a cynical, devious world we live in. It's like *Dangerous Liaisons* with hoodies.

First off, I'm not that happy with the way you spend a good seventy per cent of your email justifying your own behaviour whilst dismissing poor old Balthazar's defence case with an unreliable witness account. And yes I do maintain Fat Gareth to be an unreliable witness ever since he told me he saw Mischa Barton in High Wycombe Peacocks. Why on earth would Mischa Barton go into High Wycombe Peacocks when there's a perfectly good Top Shop next door?

Everyone knows 'Balthazar' can't handle his drink. One and a half glasses is enough for him. He's not known as Cadbury's Dairy Milk for nothing.

Granted that Tuesday night in the car park behind Tesco's isn't as romantic a location as the fruit machine next to the toilets at the Fat Goose, but those orange foglights give everything a Danny Boyle-esque street cred that might arouse urban passions, and the atmosphere there ain't too bad now they've taken away the Mosquito teen repeller thing they had. So why shouldn't Balthazar be given the same excuses you gave yourself after sucking face with the only person involved in this bedroom farce whose name you 'forgot' to give me?

Second off, why is everybody so keen to rat everyone else out here? There's more grassing up going on than re-turfing day at Wembley. Talk to Balthazar, let him off the hook as long as you both agree to keep any future extra-curricular fumbling secret from the Fat Gareths of this world, as well as from each other.

And for those of you shocked by this advice please bear in mind that we're talking about an occasional quick snog. No one's getting pregnant here, no one's getting divorced. Let's not forget we're still teenagers and we're allowed to screw up from time to time.

Screw *up*, I said.

Love

MU

Is it Just Me? Corner:

Cheryl and I have been watching this slightly disturbing new show from the US on BBC Switch. It's called *Ten Years Older*. It's about pre-teen girls getting makeovers to make them look older. Cheryl loves it. I think it's quite funny, and the producers take this 'Oh-my-God-aren't-these-girls-ghastly?' approach to head off accusations that they're responsible for the ghastlification in the first place. But I can't help thinking in my head the whole time I'm watching: Thisiswrongthis iswrongthisiswrong. Am I turning into a grumpy old woman? Since when did I develop morals? Oh God, am I turning into Jocasta?

Cheryl is the ideal TV-buddy. She lets me handle the remote, on the theory that we're going to like the same stuff anyway and she can always Sky Plus her programmes and watch them when I'm at school. Which brings me to the question, what does she do all day?

She's so much more relaxed than my mum, who has totally different theories on telly than I do. Mum, like a lot of people, labours under the misapprehension that there's Good TV and Bad TV. According to her, everything she watches (*Springwatch*, *Six Feet Under* and *Deal or No Deal*) is Good TV. Everything I watch (*Big Brother*, *The Apprentice*, anything with Gok in it) is Bad TV. It's not enough for her to just not like *Big Brother* and to just not watch it. She's angry about its very existence. She'd ban it if she could.

My argument is that it's *all* Bad TV, or at least it's all TV. Everyone defends their programme and says everyone else's programmes are drivel.

'What about *Six Feet Under*?' Mum says. Well don't get me started. That programme just proves my point, it's mindless.

You have this team of overpaid writers doing nothing

but sitting in a flash office in Hollywood, writing and rewriting over and over to get the lines just perfect while researchers, focus groups, marketing men and ratings-watchers feed back to them incredibly detailed sets of data about which part of their audience likes this joke and how many people switched off at the gay kiss and exactly how much quirkiness they should put in and what percentage should be original and what percentage should be exactly the same as every other mindless US drama series that everyone said was ground-breaking at the time but now has just slipped into this featureless melange of dated haircuts and alcoholic actors.

None of it's any good, ultimately. None of it's real, none of it happens by accident. And before you say it, yes I know even the reality stuff is scripted these days. But sometimes they forget their lines and do something original and wonderfully stupid. That's maybe a little more ranting than you were looking for today, and all simply to justify my choice to watch *Big Brother* rather than an arthouse film on BBC4.

OK, OK, enough about TV. It's my party tonight. I'm so excited, though not as excited as Cheryl who's bouncing about like a hyperactive toddler in an oxygen tent. She's got caterers and decorators in today fixing the place up. Dad's staying at his crash-pad in London, which is very wise I must say.

'Do you think we should have more balloons?' she asked me when I came into the kitchen to get some toast. 'I have a friend who runs a circus school, should I get some jugglers?'

'Yes, and yes,' I said. Not wanting to seem anything less than enthusiastic.

'Really?' she asked, looking frantic, then rushed off to find her phone.

'Actually no!' I shouted after her. 'I mean balloons yes, jugglers no.'

I thought I'd better get out of there before she decided we might need a clown. I went down to the village to see Jugs. She was still ignoring my calls, and even though Sonia Bailey had told me Jugs was definitely coming to the party, I wanted to make sure we were cool before then. I didn't want us to be shooting daggers back and forth the whole night.

Jugs lives in a tiny cottage, like a Mr Men house, with her mum. Her dad is absent without leave and we're not allowed to talk about him. Her mum's lovely but a bit of a natterer and I didn't fancy being force-fed shortbread and a gallon of tea so I slipped around the back, being careful not to tread on the tulips. I chucked a pebble up at Jugs's window and after a while she poked her dark-haired head out. When she saw it was me her nostrils flared but she stayed where she was.

'Hello,' she said.

'Hello,' I said.

'Nice of you to pop by,' she said.

'Your phone seems to be broken,' I told her. 'You probably didn't realize, what with never getting any calls anyway, but there you are.'

'My phone works fine, actually,' she said. 'I've been getting so many calls and texts that I have to filter out the ones from people who aren't genuine friends.'

'Oh I see,' I said. 'It must be difficult having so many friends.'

'It is. The waiting list is very long.'

'How do you get on the waiting list?' I asked.

She thought for a while. 'You have to invent a cocktail in my honour.'

'A cocktail? What should it have in it?'

'You decide.'

'OK, what should it be called, this cocktail of forgiveness?'

'Again, that's up to you. But it had better be good.'

'OK, it will.' I grinned. 'Can you come out now?'

She shook her head. 'I have an essay, and I reckon I won't feel like doing it tomorrow. See you tonight though, yeah?'

I nodded. 'Seeya.'

'Oh, hold on,' she said as I turned to leave.

'Yeah?'

'I presume Poop is going to be there tonight?'

I nodded, looking up at her, with her ample boobs resting comfortably on the sash. She's very pretty, Jugs. Poops is such an idiot for letting her go.

'OK, I can live with that,' she said, 'but please don't try and . . . engineer a reconciliation, will you?'

Of course the entire point of the party was to engineer a reconciliation, so I just gave her a WTF? look.

'I mean, don't try and arrange things so that he and I end up sat next to each other, and don't let's play spin-the-bottle,' she said, sighing.

'Spin-the-bottle? This isn't *Sweet Valley High*.'

'You know what I mean,' she huffed. 'Just don't do your usual match-making thing. Stop trying to run everything.'

I nodded and smiled, all the time thinking: But that's what I do.

Walking home with a Big Gulp from the village shop, I thought about what she'd said. What's wrong with trying to encourage people to get together? If two people are suited to each other, then why not give them a little push? Sometimes they need it. People are happier when they're in a couple, and it's better for the rest of us too. Back in the day it was all perfect, when we all lived here in Clifton, in the old house, and all my mates were here and Jugs and Poop were a Constant Couple and everyone

167

knew where they were. What was wrong with wanting that back again?

I'm tired, but time for a couple of emails. This one's for the Follow-Up Corner:

(via text)
YO! MISSUNDERS

IT BE GEX HERE AGAIN INNIT. WATCH OUT!

ME AND ME GIRL IS GOING TO LONDON TO SEE A BRITISH 50 CENT TRIBUTE ACT CALLED 25 PENCE. IT WON'T FINISH TILL WELL-LATE AND I WANNA GET A HOTEL AND TREAT HER RIGHT ALL NIGHT BUT I'M A BIT SHORT ON CASH INNIT. ANY ADVICE, BRUV?

GEX

Hi Gex
To judge by the more confident tone in your email I'm guessing things have moved on since your last request for help. I don't want to know the sordid details though, so please let's leave it at that.

I'm not entirely sure what you're asking me here. Do you want me to recommend cheap accommodation in the London area? In which case I'd point you in the direction of the electric internet. Or are you asking for assistance in how to go about seducing this girl? I'm guessing the latter, and do you want to know for why? Because my friend Blingirrl with the lop-sided boobs knows who you are and has informed me that far from being the streetwise gangsta you claim to be, you are in fact Mr Geeky McPaleface and are thought to be – how can I put this delicately – a little inexperienced, shall we say?

Look dude. Forget the hotel, just make sure you catch the last train, try to find a double-seat in a carriage without sick all over the seats. Then once you've set off, open your bag and suprise her with a romantic little picnic. Sandwiches, crisps, chocolate. Maybe even a miniature bottle of her favourite tipple. (Do they do Cherry Lambrini in miniature?) She'll love it. Walk her home from the station. If she's really into you, she might invite you in. If not, give her a kiss on the cheek and call her the next day.

It's not rocket science. Just don't expect too much, too soon, get me?

Miss Unders

Dear Miss Understanding
My boyfriend told me that he loved me last night. What's that all about? We've only had three dates and they're not even really dates cos we just hang about on the swings in the playground at Moswell Park.

He looked well-shamed afterwards and started

showing me his phone. He's got the new rzr which is well cool and you can put a thousand MP3s on it or half an hour of happy-slaps.

What should I do? Stick or twist?

Hugsy

Dear Hugsy

Hmmm. I didn't know what to think until you mentioned he had the rzr. Has he downloaded Hamburglar 4 yet? It's very challenging, especially the Nacho Boss on level two, he can be a little unpredictable.

Now where were we? Oh yes, stick or twist. Definitely stick. He sounds nice. And don't mention the 'I love you' thing. It probably just slipped out. And it's a good thing, right?

Luvs

Miss Understanding.

That's all for now. Must get plucking!

Miss Understanding Blog Entry
– 11th April 2010

OK, I'm writing this the day after the party. Wow! Is all I can say. Wow, wow, wow. I did not expect *that* to happen. Let me start at the beginning.

The party was supposed to start at 8.30 but people started turning up from 7.30. Crumpet arrived first.

'I was hungry,' she said. 'I wanted to get here before all the miniature hamburgers had been eaten.'

Poops, Jake and their friend Si turned up soon after in search of alcohol. When I'd told them there was free beer, they'd assumed that meant a can of warm lager each. I showed them the bar area set up in the dining room and they practically fainted with gratitude.

They helped me design Jugs's cocktail. It's harder than it sounds making a cocktail. You can't just pour loads of crap in together. There are rules. You can't mix brown and white for a start. You shouldn't really mix mixers either and, as Poop-chute found to his cost, you shouldn't ever put Greek yoghurt in *any* cocktail. Even the Zorba.

Eventually we settled on gin (because all good cocktails have gin in them), vermouth (because it seemed a little exotic and mysterious – like Jugs) and grapefruit juice (because Poop said grapefruits reminded him of Jugs). We called it the Bitter Martini.

Cheryl was all over the place, bossing everyone around like Angelica out of *Rugrats*. She'd got the patio heaters out again and had taken the precaution of covering over the ponds with big metal panels. The place looked fantastic. We're not just talking cheesy wotsits and a prawn ring on a collapsible table. This was a major buffet, an ice swan, a butter goose and a taramasalata chicken. Just kidding, but there was charcuterie, salads and slow-cooked belly pork.

As people arrived they came shuffling in, shy, like they were coming for an audition, but Cheryl made them all feel at home. She sat them down, got them drinks and told them to treat the place like it was theirs. Jugs arrived just after nine and we gave each other a quick hug. She even said hi to Poop and I thought everything might just turn out OK.

It didn't take long for the party to get into full swing. We played poker for pound coins, we laughed till beer came out of our noses, we argued over the music until Cheryl put one of the catering staff in charge of the stereo and banned anyone else from touching it. We invented dances and stupid forfeit games. Isobel had to run around the house with no top on. Jez had to pinch Cheryl's bottom.

Everyone loved Cheryl. She was everywhere, flirting with the boys, gossiping with the girls, discussing music and TV and boys and hair. She held Carli's hair back when she threw up in the downstairs loo, then got her coffee and let her sleep it off in her own bed.

She showed us a cool drinking game called Beerhunter, where you get ten cans, someone shakes one of them up madly, then you mix them all up and take turns cracking the cans open under your chin, like Russian Roulette. Of course when you get the shaken-up one it explodes in your face.

When some of the boys were planning a trip down to the shop to get cigarettes, Cheryl stopped them and sent one of the waiters instead. It was the perfect party really. Until it all went horribly wrong of course.

Around 11.30 The Boy turned up, looking pre-rehab Pete Doherty and accompanied by two of his rough-looking mates, who hadn't been invited. Cheryl was really good about it and let them stay as long as they promised to keep out of trouble. But it wasn't long before they disappeared out the back and we started to smell marijuana. Cheryl had to go and ask them to stop and they were a bit grumpy about it. I went to speak to The Boy about it.

'Hey you,' I said, 'nice of you to dress up.'

He peered down at himself. 'I suppose I am looking a little slipshod,' he said. 'Want me to pop home and get my dress Crocs? These ones are a little manky.'

'No, you look fine, just keep an eye on your mates, OK? No smoking weed here tonight, got it?'

'OK Buxton,' he said, grinning at me in a way that made me feel both square and childish. But I gave him a stern look and walked off.

Anyway it all settled down again after a while, but I still had this bad feeling, like there was a fat rain cloud over my perfect fairy picnic. Crumpet and Belle and I were trying to do some of the routines from *Step Up 2* when someone mentioned that The Boy and his mates had disappeared. I figured they'd probably be in the garden smoking again so went to have a look.

It was still and mild and beautiful outside, the moon was nearly full and I had no trouble seeing where I was going. I walked between the stone willies and out towards the little summer house, from where I thought I'd heard voices.

'OK, what's going on?' I said in a mock-cop voice as I leaped around the entrance, only to stop, frozen in shock.

There, sitting on the stone bench in the summer house were The Boy and Jugs, in what can only be described as a clinch, she looking mortified, and he with a 'whoops-I-did-it-again' look on his trouble-making face.

I'm afraid I didn't handle it very well. I may have called her a fat-breasted tart in fact. I didn't even look at *him*.

I rushed back to the house and straight into my room and locked the door.

Cheryl found me eventually. She knocked and called through the door. 'Is everything OK?'

'No,' I said. I told her what had happened. She was silent for a while.

'Do you want me to get rid of everyone?'

I really did, but I also didn't want to ruin the night, and I knew Cheryl was enjoying herself. I didn't want her to miss out on this amazing party she'd organized and paid for.

'No, I don't want to spoil everyone's fun,' I said in a tone that let her know exactly how brave and selfless I was being.

'I'm going to wrap it up out there,' Cheryl said. 'I'll come and bring you a hot chocolate when everyone's gone, OK?'

I was so grateful I welled up.

I don't know how she got everyone to leave so quickly, but half an hour later she came back in with two cups of hot chocolate and a pack of jammy dodgers.

We sat on my bed, she took a big bite of a biscuit and said, 'I'm glad you're here, Anya.'

'I'm glad I'm here too,' I said. 'Thanks for my party, I'm sorry I ruined it.'

'You didn't ruin it, sweetie, it was Jugs and The Boy responsible for that.'

'Still, it was a wonderful party, you worked so hard.'

She looked at me and sipped her drink.

'You deserve it, Anya. And it's clear to me your mother would never have done something for you like this.'

What on earth made her go and say something like that? Why bring my mother into it? It's true of course, Mum would never think to arrange a party for me – if she did she wouldn't be able to afford caterers and she'd try to feed everyone wholewheat pasta, and she'd make a total mess of it. But this isn't a competition, is it? Cheryl and Mum are different.

'Well,' I said, feeling I had to make some kind of response to that, 'Mum is very busy.'

Cheryl snorted. 'Busy doing what?' she asked.

I had to think. 'She does a lot of charity work.'

'Yes, you don't have to be very good at charity work, do you?' and she laughed her little tinkly laugh and for an instant I wanted to slap her and shout, 'That's my mum you're talking about! And what are you doing with your life that's so goddamn important?' But instead I laughed along with her, only for it to come out a bit fake.

I put my cup down. 'Gosh, so tired,' I said.

Cheryl seemed to realize she'd gone too far. She jumped up and fussed about, moving the tray and smoothing my bed spread down. 'Yes of course,' she said. 'Now try not to worry about what happened tonight; plenty of other fish in the sea, in fact Seth was asking after you the other day, maybe I should get him over for dinner soon?'

As fanciable as Seth was, I so didn't feel up to taking part in Cheryl's little match-making experiment. Nonetheless I found myself nodding enthusiastically – anything to get her out the door.

So there I was, lying in bed, trying to make sense of it all. By rights the brain should have been replaying the HD version of the Boy-Jugs traitor-snog over and over again, but instead I found myself alternating between that and anger at Cheryl insulting my mum, along with a little dollop of nervous expectation about seeing Seth again. What's wrong with me? Why can't I be in agony about just one thing at a time?

Miss Understanding Blog Entry
– 15th April 2010

My cupboard is now so full I couldn't possibly fit any more into it. As I slammed it shut the last time, after shoving in a traffic cone Poops had brought me, I felt like a tonne of crap inside shift and fall against the door. Next time I open it the whole lot's going to come down on me. I can't remember exactly what's in there, but there's at least one antique typewriter that weighs a tonne; kind of like the one James Caan crushes Kathy Bates's skull with in *Misery*.

If I wanted to kill myself, that's how I'd do it. I'd lock all the doors, then engineer a heavy typewriter falling on my head. That'd stump the detectives.

Hey Miss U
Some friends of mine want to start a gang. This is so dumb. The closest we get to urban warfare round here is when Mr

Clark saw us drawing on the pavement with chalk and gave us a drive-by telling off.

I told them we already have a sort-of gang – a gang of friends, and they looked at me like I had brain damage. Anyway Damien got a knife the other day and everyone's talking about defending our patch. I think they mean Clematis Court but apart from the pizza guy no other teenagers ever come here except Mrs Franks's grandson – and he's not exactly on the Crips's waiting-list, what with his eczema.

I don't want to lose my friends but they're just being stupid.

BigKev

Dear Kev

I don't know, this country's gone to hell in a hand-cart. Full of tombstoning hoodies stabbing each other for crack money.

Look it's a serious issue, and I'm not the right person to comment, OK? But if you want to direct your gang's energy towards more positive endeavours than knifing Mrs Franks's grandson then why not start a hip-hop crew? Download Garageband, lay down some humming tracks. The leisure centre does hip-hop classes on Sunday mornings. I dare say your parents would be only too happy to shell out if it gets you off the streets (or the cul-de-sac in your case).

Your idiot friends can indulge their urban youth culture obsession and you can avoid ten years in chokey for stabbing the pizza guy. Everyone wins.

Especially the pizza guy.

Much love

Miss Understanding

Dear Miss Understanding
I'm worried about my friend. She's losing weight but too much and I think she might have a problem. She was always the chubby one in our posse, a bit big, you know tall and heavy, and no one ever paid much attention to her, then she lost some weight and everyone said you look well-good. And I think that got her thinking that people would like her more if she kept losing weight, so she did and now she looks like Paula Radcliffe with dysentery.

How can I help my friend?

Rosa

Dear Rosa
Honestly, I think I should give up on you people sometimes. Did you read what you wrote to me? The answer to your questions is there, in black and white, before your very eyes.

'She was always the chubby one in our posse ... no one ever paid attention to her ... people would like her more

180

if she kept losing weight . . .'

You see it yourself, then you ask me what you can do about it? I don't know the girl, but maybe she thinks she can gain popularity by losing weight. According to Mum's *Look* magazines that's a common feature of eating disorders.

You said *no one ever paid attention to her*. Well why not? She's supposed to be your friend isn't she? Sounds like she needs to build her self-confidence.

Here's what I'd do. Phone her up and ask her if she wants to go to the cinema with you to watch a girlie-flick. Then have a bite to eat in a café (not BigBurger, go somewhere you can get something healthy) and chat to her. Don't talk about food, or fashion or that sort of thing, just chat to her about normal stuff. TV, films, books, school, which boys you fancy.

Don't tell her she looks thin, don't tell her she looks fat. Just be her friend. That's all she really wants. Don't try to tackle her eating issue, that's something for her, her parents and her doctor to sort out. It'll be a lot easier for her if she has supportive friends who don't make it an issue the whole time.

Love

MU

Dear Miss Understanding,

Every summer my parents take me to their place in Spain,

which is a bit shit, really. It's near Gibraltar and is full of people exactly like my parents. I love my parents, but funnily enough I sort of don't at all love people exactly like them who aren't my parents, if you know what I mean.

They spend eleven months of the year in England moaning about how crap England is these days and one month in Spain complaining about the Spanish and shovelling full English breakfasts down their throats.

Thing is, I've got this new girlfriend and I want to stay here with her. I'm seventeen now, how can I convince them I'm responsible enough to be left on my own?

Yours

Dan

Hi Dan

Listen very carefully, I shall type this only once.

1) Don't under any circumstances mention the girl. Your parents will not be sympathetic. At all. They do not want you to go out with anyone, they do not want you to be happy, they do not want you to lead an independent life. You have to trick them. Don't feel bad about this, it's the best thing for everyone concerned.

2) Don't, under any circumstances, suggest to them that you are in any way averse to the idea of going to Spain with them for the summer. Refer to it often

and enthusiastically. 'Ooh, looking forward to those breakfasts at Fat Joe's Caff,' you should say. 'Bloody hell, this country's full of foreigners, I'm looking forward to getting to Spain so I can find someone who speaks English!' That sort of thing.

3) Get a job. Could be anything. Flipping burgers, selling shoes, anything. Make sure your parents know you don't particularly like the work, but reluctantly hint that you find it rewarding and challenging.

4) Two weeks before you leave for Spain, casually mention to your parents that you might be in line for a promotion, only you won't be applying because you're off to Spain (woohoo!) in a few weeks and think you might chuck the job in anyway.

5) Act disappointed and sullen when they demand that you stay in England to further your burger-flipping career. Sulk and slam a few doors.

6) Eventually accept their superior wisdom and wave them off tearfully at the airport.

7) Chuck your job and invite the girl over for a *Heroes* box-set session and some popcorn.

Next!

Miss Understanding

Miss Understanding Blog Entry
– 16th April 2010

Well Blogpals, today I bit the bullet and handed in my application to move back to Clifton College. Don't take it personally guys. It's not you, it's me.

Well it's some of you as well, but most of you make me want to stay, it's not been an easy decision to make. 'What has Clifton got that we don't?' I hear you ask, plaintively.

For a start it's quieter, by which I mean there's less screaming. Sometimes Woodyatt does sound a bit like a Miley Cyrus concert in the seventh circle of Hell (supp. James Blunt). And that's just during Assembly. Also Clifton has fewer knife incidents, unless you count nose-jobs, and the main problem in the loos here is people throwing up rather than people shooting up. I'm only joking! I know Allerton's not that bad and Clifton really isn't that good. It's kind of dull compared to Allerton. Plus class sizes are smaller so it means the teachers all know your name, which is never a good thing.

Look, it might never happen. They may well reject it this late in the year, even with the compassionate grounds I added on the extra sheet they grudgingly told me I could use. It's not just the fact that Cheryl is getting a little sick of driving me, and the taxi bills are starting to add up, and they've cancelled a couple of bus services meaning I really need to peg it to catch the last bus. We'll see.

Dear Miss Understanding.

It's me, Big Kev. Gangland survivor. I just wanted to let you know that my mates thought the hip-hop band was a great idea. Jeremy's dad is letting us use his garage and Sunil's dad has an old PA system from when he was in a band called the Twinkles who did kids' parties. We couldn't get the Flowertots stickers off the side so we spray-painted vomiting skulls over them. We've bought a DVD called *Rapid Breakz* and we're teaching ourselves the moves. We've made some great tracks from Garageband and I reckon we're actually pretty good.

Problem is the name. The first rehearsal we had we just sat about for four hours suggesting stupid names and still couldn't decide.

Here are some of the better suggestions:

Blakk Crew

Kid Brothers

Hipzterz

Boyz in the Close

Biggie Shouts

Wotevva Treva

See what I mean?

We've now come up with a temporary name: Blakk Solze
— because Damien reckons we are all a bit black inside you
know and also we painted the soles of our shoes black and at
the end of our final track we do this move where we all end
up on the floor with our feet stuck out in different positions
showing off our black soles. Only problem is this spray paint
is dissolving the rubber a bit and now our feet keep sticking
to the floor and we all make this sort of *skrip skrip* sound
when we walk about.

This is a shout-out to all Miss Understanding readers, we
need your help to come up with a good hip-hop name. We're
looking for alternate-spelling, maybe a little bit nonsensical
and definitely bigging us up.

Hope you can help!

Booyah!

Kev

Well there you go, readers, that's your weekly shopping
challenge. Find a good name for Big Kev's hip-hop band
and you could win a year's supply of boys' trainers (slight
sole damage).

Dear Miss Understanding

Hi, it's me, Barrelgirl again.

Well that didn't go well. I've been dumped. Double-dumped. I took Josh to a club the other night and gave him the 'I-need-some-space' speech. Then I gave him a goodbye snog.

Now somehow, I don't know how, but Max found out about this. When I went to see him yesterday he confronted me about it. He started going on about me putting myself about in public and pictures being splashed on the internet. I tried to explain that it was over with Josh and that I'd chosen him, but it sounded a bit weak. He said he was disappointed that I hadn't felt able to tell him the truth from the beginning. But how could I?

Anyway so now I'm left with neither of them.

What a mess.

Love

Barrelgirl

Dear Barrelgirl

I'm so sorry. Whoever's responsible for spilling the beans should be staked out naked in the high street on a Friday night, smeared in kebabs. Why do people do things like that?

Oh well, plenty more fish in the sea, or if men are more to your taste, plenty more men in Zeon.

Hang in there girl,

Love MU

PS Did Max say where on the internet he'd seen these pictures?

Watched *Property Ladder* with Cheryl last night, she loves anything to do with property and making money. Why don't people listen to Sarah Beeny? I mean, why go on the show if you're just going to knock through that wall and turn the upstairs bathroom into a 'meditation space' anyway? You always know how things are going to turn out, because the smug voice-over always says, 'I hope that decision doesn't come back to haunt them . . .'

To: <u>Crumpet@notmail.com</u>
Hey Crumps,
What a weird night I just had! I'm writing this from Mum's so I won't be able to come over to back-comb your hair tonight after all. (You know, I'm not sure it's such a good idea in any case. Personally I think big hair is over.)

About 11.30 pm last night, I was in bed with the telly on but drowsing, when my mobile went. I couldn't find it in the bedclothes at first as I was so groggy, but eventually I picked it up and saw it was Mum's landline. I answered it, thinking she must have locked herself out or set fire to something again and was calling to ask me what the number was for the emergency services.

But it wasn't Mum, it was Marley!

'Hey, chief,' he says.

'What's wrong, Marley, are you OK?' I asked.

'We've got a big problem,' he said and hung up on me. I called back but the phone was engaged. Tried mum's mobile but she never has it switched on, or charged up for that matter. I was in a total panic. Dad and Cheryl are in New York, there are no buses this time of night, I couldn't afford a cab. But I needed to get home. There was nothing else for it so I grabbed the keys to Cheryl's Beemer. Well, it's only twenty miles and if I drove on the back roads there was no way I was going to get caught by the Old Bill. Anyway, it was an emergency, I was sure Cheryl would be OK with it under the circumstances.

I got in, started it up and tried to remember all the things Cheryl had been teaching me. Clutch, into first, depress clutch, feel it engage, press to . . . oh shit, check your mirrors, press down on the accelerator, move off, pick up speed, clutch again, shift into second, *crunch*, out the gate, indicate, check for traffic, turn, off down the road, Christ, forgot the headlights! Clutch, third gear, and so on for twenty hair-raising miles.

When I got home I turned into the driveway a bit too fast and nearly lost control. Managed to avoid slamming into the front of the house by yanking the wheel hard across and driving into a rhododendron instead, turns out it's a very forgiving plant. That would have to do. I leaped out and raced round the back to the kitchen door, which as you know is never locked, and burst in to find the most extraordinary sight.

Mum was sat at the table, Marley to her right, schoolbooks open in front of them. They were absolutely fine, the picture of domestic bliss and most incredibly of all – *Mum was helping him with his homework!*

They looked up in astonishment at my flushed face. I suddenly felt like the biggest idiot on the planet. 'Is everything all right?' I asked.

They looked at each other. Mum shrugged and nodded. 'Yes, I think so, what's wrong with you?'

'I got a call from Marley,' I explained. 'He said you had a big problem.'

Marley shook his head. 'I didn't call you.'

Everyone looked at each other in mystification for a while until Mum remembered Marley had been messing with her phone earlier. 'He was playing *Doctor Who*,' she said. 'That was his impression of Matt Smith. He must have pressed speed-dial by mistake.'

I was annoyed, but relieved nothing was wrong, I made hot chocolate and sat down to help them decipher the code of the four times multiplication table. It looked like Mum and I had decided upon an unspoken truce.

Though eventually she said, 'How did you get here, by the way?'

I told her about the emergency requisitioning of the Beemer. Mum stared at me as if I'd just told her I'd shot Carol Vorderman. 'We'll talk about this later,' she said coldly, glancing at Marley meaningfully.

I took him upstairs later, helped with his bath and read to him for a while – he and mum were halfway through Harry Potter V. For some reason Marley took against Ron Weasley early in the series and now snorts and rolls his eyes in aggravation every time the poor red-headed wizard is mentioned. 'Come on Weasley,' he'd grumble, 'you've broken your wand *again*? Idiot!'

I went back downstairs, took a deep breath and walked back into the kitchen. Mum was standing by the sink, looking out into the dark garden. 'Have you forgotten what happened two years ago?' she asked.

'No Mum, I haven't forgotten,' I said. In a way I was OK about having this discussion. I wanted Mum to talk about it. She generally just referred to it as the lamp-post incident and refused to go into further details.

'I nearly died, because I was being an idiot.'

'I know,' I said.

'It's not my own life that's so important,' she said, 'but think of Marley.'

I blinked. What about me? Why not think of me?

I waited for her to say it, but she didn't.

'Maybe it's time you started thinking of other people,' she said.

'I *was* thinking of other people,' I protested. 'I was thinking of you and Marley. I was thinking about the claw-handed swamp-man who was tearing your limbs from their sockets and beating you with the wet bit. That's why I took the car. I had no choice.'

'Why not phone Mrs Horton?' she asked. Mrs Horton is our neighbour. 'You have her number on your phone, I saw you put it in.'

This was a good point, but I was determined to protect the heroic self-image I'd created. 'I couldn't drag poor old Mrs Horton into this, what would she do against Swamp-Man, hurl her mahjongg tiles at him?'

'If you were genuinely concerned, you should have called the police rather than risking your own life and the lives of other road users,' she said, sounding like Jamie Theakston off of *Police, Camera, Action*.

I sighed loudly and she snapped.

'You broke the fucking law, Anya!' she said.

I stood up, furious. 'You don't give a toss about the law unless it suits you,' I shouted. 'You've been arrested dozens of times, you told me yourself about all the demos you got banged up for. The time you vandalized the police van, the time you defaced that statue.'

'Those issues were important,' she said. 'They were important to me. I was prepared to risk jail.'

'And my family's important to me,' I countered. 'I don't like having two houses, two families. I don't like feeling like this, feeling split.'

She was silent then. I hadn't really meant to say that, it just jumped out. She watched me for a minute or so. Finally she said, 'You can talk to me about these things you know.'

I fixed her gaze, ignoring the tears coming, inexorably fighting their way up from my chest.

'And you can talk to me about that night, you know,' I countered. 'You can tell me what really happened.'

Then she looked dreadfully sad and shook her head. 'I'm not ready Anya, I'm sorry.'

'Were you drunk?' I asked. She just glared at me and didn't answer.

'Good night Mum,' I said, and walked out. That was that.

Oh God, Crumps, what a mess we all are. Sorry to lay this all on you, but Jugs and I still aren't talking, and there's no one else, you know.

Love, An

PS Now Wed morning. Got up just now, looked out the window into the front garden and screamed.

Cheryl's car has gone!

Miss Understanding Blog Entry
– 16th April 2010

Starting to regret staying here in Allerton until the weekend.

It's currently 4.27 am on Friday morning and Mum wasted no time in exploiting the free babysitter and going out last night, presumably with Lance, but she won't talk about him to me. Now I can't get back to sleep after being woken an hour ago by Mum returning, the worse for wear. It sounded like she fell into the sink after climbing through the kitchen window, our usual method for gaining access when we've lost keys. She then began playing Shania Twain at top volume in the living room. I stumped downstairs and gave her a look.

'Sorry, darling,' she said, slurring slightly. 'Forgot you were home actually.' I clamped her huge, old-fashioned headphones on over her silly, woofy hair and installed her in her swing-seat with a cup of coffee. She looked like an Ewok in a Death Star gun turret.

I wandered back upstairs and tried to get back to sleep, but found 'That Don't Impress Me Much' playing loop on the iPod in my head so I got up and decided to write to you lot. Gotta say that the playlist on my headPod is currently irritating beyond measure. Currently it looks like this:

Track 1) The tune from the new Head and Shoulders ad by Unknown.

Track 2) *Crying Blood* by V V Brown

Track 3) *The Fresh Prince of Bel-Air Theme* by Will Smith.

Shania's almost a welcome new addition.

I said *almost*. Been thinking over the lyrics to that song: 'That don't impress me much' says Shania, coming across as a little hard-to-please. 'So you're Brad Pitt?' she tells us. 'That don't impress me much.'

Why not, Shania? Why don't that impress you much? He's well-fit, a multi-millionaire, a great dad, an incredibly talented actor and by all accounts a really nice down-to-earth bloke. What else, exactly, are you looking for in a man? Undercarriage like an A380 Airbus and a fetish for cleaning the oven?

Not much point going back to bed now, Marley will be up in half an hour. Might try and write an essay. L8rs.

ANYABABE! WTF? WTG ALL DAY TO FIND OUT STORY WITH CH'S
CAR? RU IN JAIL? PSE, EMAIL/TXT/PHONE ME – CRUMPS

SHIT! SOZ BOUT THAT, FORGOT TO TELL U. MUM GOT LANCE
TO DRIVE CH'S CAR BACK TO C'TON LAST NITE. V RELIEVED, BUT
NARKED NOT YET INTRODUCED TO RAMBLING LANCE. L8RS. A

Miss Understanding Blog Entry
– 17th April 2010

Loads of responses to Kev's appeal for band names. Some better than others. Jenna Hall suggests Boy-hop, which to me sounds like the sort of thing Julian Clary might get up to in the privacy of his own home. Guy DuLancey came up with MC Kev feat. N@ J, which is OK, but looks a little too much like a web address. Closer to genius is Bluegrass who suggests MC Middle-Klass, but I think Myleene might sue.

No, the winner, for me, has to be Bonnie Greaves's entry, with Biggie Kev and the C-street Massive. I look forward to the inevitable set at the end-of-term dance and shall expect props to me.

Despite all the bonding Marley and Mum have been doing while I've been away, he hasn't been eating well. I'm sure he's lost weight. The fridge is full of non-digestible ready-meals in non-biodegradable packaging. In a vain effort to get him to eat something real (he was nearly sick when I told him where eggs come from) I've been doing some recipes from a Gordon Ramsay book. They're soooo frustrating. You think you're doing really well, following all the instructions to the letter, then all of a sudden he throws you by saying something like: 'Now add the tapenade (page 176),' and you turn to page 176 and it tells you you need Greek olives, which you completely don't have, and that you should have been marinating since February.

Couldn't help but notice the freezer is full of banoffee pie, but there ain't no cheesecake for li'l ole me. Must be a relief for Mum not to have to go all the way over to Sainsbury's these days.

Dear Miss Understanding
Do I have to wear a condom if all we're doing is oral?
Yours
JH

Dear JH,
These days, you even have to wear a condom if all you're doing is Wii tennis.
Luv
Miss Understanding

Dear Miss Understanding

I think my boyfriend might be cheating on me. I said I wanted to wait until I was eighteen before I had sex. He was really disappointed and kept on at me all the time. Then all of a sudden he stopped asking me to sleep with him. At the same time he started hanging around with his 'friend' Susie all the time. I think they're more than just friends. She just blanks me at school and her mates go quiet when I walk past.

I've asked my boyfriend about her and he says they're just friends and that he wants to be with me.

Then on Friday Imogen Chivers says she saw him at BigBurger with her. They weren't kissing or anything but he'd told me he couldn't go to see *Stomp Da Yard 4* with me that night because he was staying in to finish an essay.

What do you think?

Love

Suspicious

Dear Suspicious

Hmmm, on the face of it, it really does seem that Mr Perfect might have not been behaving himself. Nice girl doesn't put out, boy seeks large-breasted floozy and goes a bit quiet on the hearts-and-flowers front. It's a tired old tale.

On the other hand you might be being a little unfair on your boyf. For a start, it could well be that Susie fancies your boyfriend and is frustrated by his refusal to dump you. If Susie was sleeping with your bloke I think she'd actually be a lot nicer to you. It's when 'the other girl' acts like your best mate that you need to start worrying. Also I'm not sure that the fact that he's stopped pestering you for sex means all that much. If he was sleeping with Susie, it wouldn't stop him wanting to have sex with you. I can't back this up with personal experience, but Mum's magazines suggest that men are quite greedy in this regard, the more they have, the more they want. Like Pringles.

And finally, his refusal to go to see *Stomp Da Yard* 4 with you means zilch. Of *course* he's not going to see *Stomp Da Yard* with you. Of *course* he's going to lie about it, he doesn't want to hurt your feelings. Everyone knows it's a shit film. (I'll go and see it with you though.)

Look, why not give him the benefit of the doubt? If he *is* sleeping around you'll probably find out sooner or later and then you can write in and tell me I'm an idiot, but for now, let's pretend the world is a fair place.

Yours,

Miss Hope-and-Understanding

Email to Al@notmail.com
Well am I red-faced or what?

I'm red faced, that's what.

Today, after double Science, Ms Cooper asked me to stay behind. Having spent most of the lesson blind-texting Crumpet under my jumper (have you ever tried it? You have to do it by memory and it generally makes no sense whatsoever but is very entertaining) I thought I knew what it would be about.

But she surprised me, she asked me to sit down, gave me a funny look and said:

'I'm Barrelgirl.'

Now I'm not sure if you've been reading the blog lately. You claim you haven't but I'm pretty sure you have. Either way, Barrelgirl is someone who wrote to me asking for my advice on which of two men she should go out with. I helped her make up her mind.

Meanwhile, I posted photos of Ms Cooper snogging some bloke at Zeon on my site. Turns out that 'Josh' is actually Mr Graves the PE teacher. I thought at the time it was a dumb idea and now I know it was, because poor old Ms Cooper has now been dumped by both of her blokes and is a tiny bit gutted, to be honest.

'But how did Max find out about them?' I asked.

'Does it matter?' she said.

'S'pose not,' I said. Then had a thought. 'Maybe Josh found them and emailed Max the link?' I suggested.

'Maybe, but this is beside the point,' she said gently.

'Sorry,' I replied. 'Oh no, that can't be it. Josh is unlikely to have had Max's email address after all.'

'Anya!' Ms Cooper said sharply. 'Forget about how it happened, I want to talk to you about what *you* did.'

'Sorry,' I said again, trying to focus.

'If you'd have known who I was, would you have posted those photos on the internet?' she asked.

'No,' I said. 'Of course not.'

'So what makes you think it's OK to do it to someone who you don't know?'

'I dunno,' I mumbled feeling like a little kid. I hate it when adults say things like that that are just so *old* and *obvious* and yet you know they're right and you can't argue.

'Are you going to shop me then?' I asked.

'What do you mean?'

'Are you going to tell Big Head who I am?'

'Oh Anya,' she laughed, 'everyone knows who you are. We have from day one.'

Now that was a little gobsmacking.

'So what were all the letters about?'

'We had to send those because we had complaints. Also we were trying to get you to tone it down a little, and maybe to get your mother to keep an eye on what you were doing.'

'Hmmphh. She doesn't care.'

'She does, I've spoken to her.'

This was turning out to be a day of surprises. 'You've spoken to Mum about me?'

'Yes, she's concerned about you, Anya.'

'Hang on. Does she read my blog?'

'No, in fact I had the greatest difficulty explaining exactly what a blog was,' Ms Cooper said. 'I tried to explain that you'd chosen to put your "diary" in the public domain, but I'm not entirely sure she understood.'

'No, she's not very . . . er, astute, in a technological sense.'

'Perhaps not.'

'Why haven't you tried to shut me down then, if you all know who I am?'

She shrugged. 'Not much we can do about you. We brought the matter to your mother's attention, but she said you were living with your father now and we should speak to him. We didn't have a number for your father so we sent him a letter. We haven't received a response.'

'Look,' I said, 'I'm really sorry about what I did. It was stupid and childish.'

'It was,' she said, 'but I was being a little childish myself, and I did appreciate your advice.'

'Thanks,' I said. 'Do you think I should stop doing the agony thing?'

'I think you're brilliant, Anya,' she said, smiling warmly. 'And I don't think you should stop.'

'Really?'

'Really, I just want to see you being a little more careful with other people's lives.'

I nodded, feeling a little choked-up. On the way out I stopped and turned back.

'I know what happened,' I said.

'What? What do you mean?' she asked.

'I know how Max came across those pictures of you on the internet.'

She rolled her eyes. 'Go on,' she said.

'He googled you. Just because he's old, doesn't mean he doesn't know how to google a new girlfriend.'

She nodded, and looked incredibly sad for a moment. 'You're probably right, Anya. He probably googled me.'

And then I left and that was that. How weird! How huge!

Love

An

PS Did I see you walking home with Saskia Petersen last night? Not jealous or anything, just want to know what you're up to. I'd like to think at least one of us is having some success in that area.

Miss Understanding Blog Entry
– 14th May 2010

Hooray! Got the place to myself and am seriously tempted to get the guys over. Maybe I'll just invite Crumpet. But for now, I need to catch up on some of the car-crash lives you love-zombies lead.

Dear Miss Understanding

My boyfriend has this really long tongue and won't stop sticking it down my throat whenever we kiss. Sometime I just try to give him a little peck and next thing I know I have this eel-thing tickling my voice-box. I try to protest but I'm too busy fighting for air.

How do I get him to rein in the mouth-squid without hurting his feelings?

Yours,

Sore Throat

Dear Sore

Oh don't talk to me about throat invasions. I was snogging with this bloke once and made the mistake of closing my eyes and opening my mouth. Wham, straight in. I thought at first he was trying to jam a seal pup in there. Someone looking at us in profile would have seen the back of my neck bulge out.

What to do? Have you considered biting it off? Harsh but effective. Don't rule it out, but first you should probably try something slightly less violent. How about the old 'accidental eavesdrop' trick. Chat with a friend (properly briefed of course) within hearing range of old tiger-tongue, big him up a bit, to make sure he's properly listening, then tell your friend the only thing you don't like about your beloved is the overactive gob-flopper.

Don't make too much of it, but make sure you explain exactly what it is about it you don't like.

Next time, he'll keep his pie-hole python firmly in its cage. And if he doesn't, then chomp the damn thing off. He can't say he wasn't warned.

Yours

MU

Dear Miss Understanding

My boyfriend likes to cook for me. I come over to his on the weekend and we babysit for his little brother and he cooks me this great food like Thai and Mexican.

Problem is, the other night I was in the bathroom just fixing my make-up and he comes in and starts peeing right there with me in the room.

'You don't mind, do you?' he says. I didn't say anything, I was too shocked. And then to make it worse, he walks out without washing his hands!

How can I eat the food of a free-pee-er who won't wash his hands?

Yours in horror

Screamqueen

Dear Screamqueen

If I was American I'd say, 'Eww! That's gross!'

But consider this; I read somewhere that the average toilet is eight times cleaner than the average kitchen surface where food is prepared.

Having said that, who wants to chop garlic on the loo seat? Not good for the spine, I've heard. So I don't know where that gets us. I'm flapping about all over the place tonight. Focus Miss U, focus!

I suggest you don't mention the whole peeing-in-front-of-you thing, I'd just try and avoid going to the bathroom when you think he might need to pee. Which, knowing most guys, is about once a day – unless they're drinking beer, in which case it's every forty seconds.

The wee-on-the-hands thing is more of a concern. It's not just the food, is it? Imagine him stroking your cheek as he's about to kiss you tenderly, you'll just be thinking about all the tiny green bugs sitting on his fingertips after recently being released from the unspeakable depths of his freaky boy-bladder.

No, you need to nip this one in the bud. Easily done. Tell him the smell of Kandoo Kids Antibacterial Hand Gel (other hand gels are available) makes you hot and buy him a super-saver-size bucket of the stuff.

Yours lavingly

Miss Understanding

Blue Sky Corner: The other day Cheryl asked me if I wanted to paint my room. I didn't really but she handed me some paint sample charts. It's one of those super-expensive poncy paint companies, as opposed to the B&Q own-brand Oatmilk Satin Sheen mum slaps on everything at home. Crikey, they have stupid names for some of these colours. Like these, from the 'Suspended Enigma' range of colours:

Intense Eggshell

Hesitant Mushroom

Cracked Wheatgrass

Quavering Orange

Sounds like breakfast in a lunatic asylum. So today I want more prosaic colour suggestions from you. Hard-nosed, tell-it-like-it-is paints. Honest, salt-of-the-earth paints. Things like Ruddy Pink, or Purple Bruise or WKD Blue.

Anyway that's all from me today,

Seeya, wouldn't wanna be ya.

Miss Understanding

Hey Anya,

How do you get yourself into these situations? And more to the point, how do you manage to get yourself out so easy? You're like the Teflon agony aunt, nothing ever sticks to you.

Gotta say you didn't really seem that cut up about screwing around with Ms Cooper's love life. I know you and I have agreed to disagree on this, and I'm not going to say I told you so, but I *did* tell you so. I know that being nice to random people isn't top of your agenda, but getting punched in the face must be a concern surely?

Anyway, lecture over. Shall we eat lunch together tomorrow? Saskia is just a friend and won't be joining us, so don't be scared off by thinking you might have to actually talk to another human being at school. In anticipation of your usual demand that we 'swap' half our lunches, I'll get Mum to make an extra sandwich as I don't fancy aduki bean salad despite what I said to you last week when I told you it was my favourite.

Love

Al

Miss Understanding Blog Entry
– 15th May 2010

Oh crap, I've really done it now. I'm back at Mum's. I think for good this time. This is not through choice, you understand, but because I kinda screwed up a little last night. Let me start at the beginning.

I thought Cheryl and Dad were returning from New York on Saturday, but when I checked the itinerary, I realized it was actually Sunday – the flight takes off on Saturday night but because of the time difference it doesn't get here until Sunday morning. So I was at a loose end. I watched TV for a while, and tried to study, but then I got bored and phoned Crumpet. She said she was going to the Bull with everyone else. No one had bothered to invite me, even though it was *Jugs* who'd been kissing The Boy. So it seems the rift in the group is healed now, after my party (good times), but now I'm not part of the group any more (bad times).

I decided I'd go along anyway. So I did. When I walked in, Jugs's face dropped like Kelly Binns's knickers at closing time. Everyone but her was glad to see me anyway, which was a relief, I was worried that my ending the party so early had put everyone's noses out of joint.

Jake got up to get me a drink, I slipped into a seat next to Poops.

'Hey, Buxton,' Poops said. 'How's your knee?'

'Oh I had it removed, it just wasn't worth it any more – what about your shoulder?'

'Turns out it wasn't my shoulder that was the problem, but my head. They took it off. Cleaned around inside with a toilet brush and that seems to have cleared things up nicely.'

Usually our I'm-sicker-than-you act got a few laughs, but right then everyone was busy being tense, waiting to see what Jugs would do.

Anyway, to cut a long story short, we all had a few drinks, and Jugs sat there and didn't say anything, and I think I may have made a couple of pointed remarks about friends, and eventually she stood up and walked out. Everyone went quiet and looked at me and eventually I said, 'Oh bollocks,' and rushed after her.

I found her outside, crying and fumbling with her phone.

'Calling him I suppose,' I said, unwisely.

'Oh screw you,' she snapped. 'Why are you here anyway? Why don't you piss off back to Allerton?'

That hurt almost as much as finding her with The Boy.

'Is that what you want? You want me out of the way so you can carry on with The Boy?'

She laughed. 'I'll carry on with The Boy if I want to, whether you're here or not,' she said. 'Fact is I don't want to and I never did. This has nothing to do with him.'

'No, it's to do with you betraying me,' I said, hating myself for sounding so pompous.

'How is it a betrayal? He's not your boyfriend.'

'No, but you know how I feel about him,' I said. Could she not see how much in the wrong she was?

'I know you keep telling me you don't feel anything for him,' she said. 'You tell us all he's just some guy you snog from time to time. You don't want him to be your boyfriend, you accept that he's with other girls.'

'Not with *you*!' I screamed. 'You deserve better than him.'

'Oh don't pretend you're concerned for me,' she snapped. She took a cigarette out of her purse and lit it, looking like a character from *Casablanca* or something. 'You pissed off to Allerton, you hardly called, you spent all your time on your stupid blog, expecting me to find out about your life the same way hundreds of strangers do.'

'It wasn't my fault I moved to Allerton, I didn't want to go.'

'Even before you moved, you didn't pay any attention to me, you just saw me and Poop as a comfortable little unit, safe and content, not worthy of your attention. You spent all your time trying to match make, or sort out people's problems, or finding out other people's business. Somewhere along the way you forgot you were supposed to be my friend.'

My God, where had all this come from?

'And that's why you snogged The Boy?' I asked. 'To get back at me?'

'Oh fuck you, Anya,' she hissed. 'You have to reduce everything to some bit of cod-psychology you learned off the internet. Not everything is some neat little problem with a cliché for a cause and a snappy one-liner for a solution.'

'So why, then?'

'Because I was sad, and he was there and he was funny and sweet. The same reasons you always end up snogging him. No reason and every reason.'

'And did you think about me, at all?' I asked.

'Funnily enough, I didn't,' she said. 'I generally don't think about you when I have some bloke's tongue down my throat. Don't be offended, will you?'

'I would have thought about you,' I lied.

214

'Oh, like you're always thinking of me when you're flirting with Poop, yeah?'

'What are you talking about?' I sputtered. But I knew exactly what she meant. Poops and I had always had a connection.

'You know, with your cute little flirtationship, and him fawning all over you. Have you ever paid for a drink yourself?'

'You're a nutter,' I said.

She stood and dropped her cigarette, ground it under her foot and turned to leave.

'That's it?' I said. 'You're just going to go?'

'Yes,' she said, stopping but not turning. It wasn't late and the low spring sun backlit her long, dark hair. 'You're just going to keep making snide remarks if I go back in there,' she sniffed. 'That's not my ideal Saturday night.'

I thought about calling her back, telling her I should be the one to go. But I was too angry. Even though I understood why she'd done it, I was still too angry. Angry at what she'd done, but also angry because I knew she was right. I had been a crap friend.

I went back in just in time for Jake to add my scrumpy to the latest round.

Later, much later I found myself back at Cheryl's. The room was spinning gently around my ears as I stood staring at my phone. When had this message come through? Two hours ago? Why hadn't I felt the thing vibrate? This stupid phone.

The message was from The Boy: *Feel really bad about wot hpnd. Can we tlk?*

With some difficulty, I texted back: *Wre RU?*

I made myself a coffee while waiting for a response, The Boy was a slow texter. I was trying to clear my spinning head. I knew what I needed to do, I needed to drink coffee, water, have a shower, then climb into bed.

But that wasn't what I *wanted* to do. I wanted to find out where The Boy was and go to him. I wanted to slap him, then kiss him. I know, I'm an idiot, so don't bother emailing to tell me. Eventually the phone buzzed.

At Cricketers, is lock-in. Can U come?

I should have played it cool. I should have waited ten minutes at least, I should have made him beg, or better yet, made him come to me. But I didn't even bother to think it over, I just typed YES, and sent it. Then I phoned a cab.

'Be about an hour this time of night, love.'

I hung up and tried two other firms, with the same result. One of them just snorted at me. 'You won't get a cab up on the hill this late on a Saturday.'

I think you can see where this is heading. Believe me, if I had been sober at that time, reading this account I'd

216

be groaning and covering my eyes and saying, 'Anya, I know what you're thinking, but for God's sake, whatever you do don't, please don't, take Cheryl's car to go and see The Boy.'

I took Cheryl's car to go and see The Boy.

Look, it's only three miles or so down to the Cricketers, in Incham. I could have walked it really, but there wasn't all the time in the world. The Boy wouldn't be coherent if I left it too much longer. There was a tiny little track I could take, no chance at all of coppers. I'd drive slowly and be back in an hour. What could go wrong?

And in fact nothing did go wrong. I made it without much difficulty, just a couple of wrong turns and an awkward moment when I knocked over someone's recycling box. I parked behind the pub, turned off the engine thankfully and banged on the kitchen door, I'd been to lock-ins here before and knew the landlord. He was an old school friend of mum's. He let me in and grinned, showing a couple of missing teeth.

'Your lad's in the snug,' he said.

'What kind of condition is he in?'

'He'll either ask you to marry him,' he said, 'or he'll bludgeon you to death with a snooker cue.'

'OK,' I said. 'Wish me luck.'

I slipped unnoticed through the bar, half visible through the haze of punters ignoring the smoking ban. I saw The Boy sitting a little awkwardly, staring at the table in front of him, a pint glass held thoughtfully between his long fingers as if it were a chess piece he was considering where to put.

'If you were one of the Mr Men, you'd be Mr Drunk,' I said, sliding into the snug opposite him.

He was so surprised to see me he spilled his beer. 'Oh bollocks,' he said.

'How much did you drink?' I asked.

He peered at the bar. 'All of it, I think.'

Then looked back at me slightly bleary-eyed and smiled. 'If you were a Little Miss, you'd be Little Miss Understanding.'

'You've told me that before. A long time ago. And what's Little Miss Understanding's story?'

He thought for a bit. 'She's always really lovely to naughty Mr Drunk. Then she finds him kissing Little Miss Saucy, or Little Miss Boobalicious . . .'

'Or Little Miss Chav?' I added.

'Hey? Oh yeah, her. And then Mr Drunk thinks she won't want to talk to him any more, but then she comes walking through the smoke and sits there looking all pretty.'

'And what makes her so understanding?' I asked.

'She's the only one who understands how sad Mr Drunk is.'

I shook my head impatiently. 'Can we lose the self-pity for now? What else does she understand?'

'That he's not good for her.'

'No, he's not,' I said. 'Not until he sorts himself out, anyway.'

'I can do that,' he said, staring at me intently. And just then, like always, I wondered if maybe he could.

'Seriously though Anya, are we cool?'

'You had me at "Oh bollocks",' I said sarcastically.

He had another gulp of beer and sat back, staring at me piteously.

'I'm going to take you home,' I said.

'Yeah?' he said, eyes popping.

'I'm going to drop you off at your house, is what I mean. Come on.'

I bundled him into the BMW and took off down towards Farringdon, the village where The Boy lives with his mother and stepsisters. He slumped in the passenger seat, flicking through my iPod and snorting with derision.

'How's the demo coming along?' I asked.

'Finished,' he said.

'Happy with it?'

'It's OK, yeah.'

'Can I hear it?'

'No.'

'Why not?'

'Because you're a better writer than I am a musician and I'd be embarrassed.'

'I am *not* a better writer than you are a musician,' I said, secretly pleased.

'Let's not start this again,' he said.

I pulled up outside the tiny council house. An old mattress had been laid carefully on top of the garden wall and bits of a motorbike littered the front garden. I'd been round once before, it was worse inside. I turned back to see him smiling and fluttering his eyelashes.

'Get out, loser,' I said.

'Fancy a coffee?'

'Hmmm, let me think, have I suddenly gone insane? No, I haven't, so no thanks.'

'Fair enough,' he said. 'The Boy doesn't beg.' He leaned over and kissed me on the cheek before I could move. And then he was out the car and disappeared around the back of the house.

I took a deep breath and started the car.

'Hello, Mum?'

'Anya? What's wrong?'

'. . .'

'Anya? Darling. What is it?'

'Mum, I've crashed Cheryl's car.'

'. . .'

'Mum?'

'My God, darling, are you hurt?'

'Oh no, I'm fine. The car has a nasty dent in it though. Cheryl's going to kill me.'

'Where are you?'

'Halfway between Farringdon and Clifton. On that little road with the white farmhouse.'

'Is the car off the road?'

'Yes, it still moves, but makes a funny noise so I thought I'd better not drive it. I pulled off to the verge.'

'How did it happen?'

'A truck came around a corner too fast, I swerved to avoid it and ran into a fence post.'

'Wait there, darling. Stay in the car, lock the doors and just wait. Will you do that for me darling?'

'Yes, Mum.'

I sat in the driver's seat, clutching the steering wheel and stared straight ahead down the road towards Clifton, and waited for my mum to come and get me.

Half an hour later I was woken up by a tapping on the window. I shrieked and looked up into the face of a man with a goatee. I shrieked again and checked the doors were still locked.

'Anya?' the goat-man called.

'Who are you?'

221

'I'm Lance,' he said. 'Your mum sent me. She's had a few drinks, see?'

'You're Welsh?' I said.

'I am,' he said.

'I didn't think you'd be Welsh.'

'Well I am Welsh,' he repeated.

'I like Welsh people,' I told him.

'OK, so will you open the door?'

'Yes I will.'

Lance told me to go and sit in his car while he checked the BMW. His wasn't the sort of car you'd expect a rambling Welsh plumber to own. You'd expect a van full of walking sticks and plumb-bobs, but it was a clean, comfortable Renault.

He climbed into the driver's seat and gave me a cheery smile.

'Don't worry love, the damage isn't bad, it's just the bumper bar's cracked and part has got lodged under the chassis. Couple of hours in the BMW garage down in Allerton.'

I sighed with relief. Cheryl would still kill me, or more likely would delegate the job to Dad, but at least I wouldn't be spending the next ten years trying to pay off the repair bill. Maybe just the summer.

Lance drove me back to Mum's place without being told. I didn't argue. Half an hour later we were back home. Mum gave me a huge hug while Lance put the kettle on. My head was just a mess of images and dread.

'I'm not going to yell,' Mum said. 'You've had a bad enough day as it is.'

I nodded. 'Thanks.'

'Besides, that's the Housekeeper's job, and your father's. Are they still away?'

I nodded again.

'OK, well we'll phone the police in the morning and report it.'

I looked up at her in horror. Was she serious?

'Do we have to do that? Could I not just arrange to pay Cheryl back for the damage?'

'You'll need a police incident report for the insurance,' Lance pointed out.

'And besides Anya, don't you think it's about time you started doing the right thing?' Mum said. 'Taking responsibility for your actions?'

I nodded for a third time. I had no energy for the fight. I was desperately tired but wasn't ready for bed, my head was just too frantic. So Mum and I sat on the couch and watched a taped episode of *Deal or No Deal*. Lance sat in the armchair, knobbly rambler's knees splayed out, like he owned the place. Everything felt surprisingly normal.

When I finally went to bed, I sent a text to Cheryl

explaining what I'd done. I didn't want her coming home and panicking about the car.

I slept for twelve hours and was finally woken by the buzzing of my phone on the bedside table.

'Hello?' I mumbled.

'Don't worry about a thing,' Cheryl chirped into my ear.

'Whassa?'

'I've picked up the car and taken it down to the garage. I'll have it back tomorrow. Your father's going to come and pick you up after lunch.'

'Aren't you mad at me?' I asked, totally confused by now.

She paused briefly. 'Your father wants to have a little chat with you, sweetie. I think that's important. I'm just glad you're OK – you are OK, aren't you?'

I thought about this for a second. 'I suppose so,' I said.

'See you soon. I've got so many photos to show you of New York, next time I'm going to insist you come.'

What will it take to break that woman, I wonder?

I could tell Mum wasn't happy, but there wasn't much she could do. If she forced me to report the incident to the police, they'd want to know why Cheryl hadn't reported it herself. Mum couldn't start a war with Cheryl without acknowledging that she had a name.

She stood there making lunch, slamming knives down, dropping butter pats on the stone floor and savagely hacking great lumps off the wheatgerm bread. I ignored her and watched Lance help Marley with his homework.

'So two numbers added up make a bigger number?' Marley asked.

'That's right,' Lance said.

'And it just keeps going up and up?'

'Yes, it does.'

'What happens if you get to the biggest number, what do you do then?'

'Good question. What do you think the biggest number is?' Lance asked.

Marley thought for ages. Eventually he said, 'Four hundred and twenty-six?'

Lance smiled. 'What about four hundred and twenty-seven?'

Marley nodded, shrugged and said, 'Oh well, I was close.'

Mum dropped a jar of wholegrain pasta on to the floor and said a word that rhymed with chuck. I thought it best to come up and write my blog.

My darlings, I'm so sorry I've been neglecting you. My tedious life has been impinging again, I know it. I'm so sorry. Your pathetic, tragic, pleading emails are building up in my inbox like clouds on a bank holiday.

Here are a couple of agonizing problems to keep you going.

Dear Miss Understanding

My girlfriend thinks it's fun to tickle me. Whenever we're alone together, and sometimes even when we're out in public, she'll kiss me, and then as soon as it gets a bit steamy, she starts giggling and trying to tickle me. If I try to stop her she sulks.

I go along with it because I know she thinks it's fun. But actually I really hate it. She's quite a 'fun' person. Do you know what I mean? Thing is she doesn't really want to do the things that I think are fun.

Am I being an arse? I know most of the girls who write in complain about boys only being interested in one thing, and I can't deny I would like to sleep with her, but if she's not ready that's fine, I just don't think that tickling is really an adequate substitute for sex.

Hoob

Dear Hoob

Hmmm. Sounds almost like she's nervous. Do you think that's at all remotely possible? That she's attracted to you but scared out of her mind at the idea of actually having sex? Gee, what are you going to do about that? How can you get this weirdo, unknowable girl into bed?

Have you thought about telling her you want to take it one step further, introducing toys such as feather dusters, or giant rubber hands?

On second thoughts maybe you should just let her know you're OK with the whole not-having-sex thing for a while as long as she agrees to stop tickling you. She's your girlfriend, blud. You are allowed to talk to her, you know?

Luv

Little Miss Tickle

Dear Miss Understanding,

My best friend Nancy is doing a first year Hairdressing NVQ and she insists on doing my hair. She doesn't charge me for it, and it's great fun chatting away and watching Jerry Springer and that while she does my highlights, but the problem is she's really crap at hairdressing. Plus she drinks a *lot* while we're doing it and I always have to go and get it fixed by a proper hairdresser the next day.

The thing is she never notices. I get back from Toni and Guy having spent £50 and I'll see Nancy and it's all, 'You look great! I'm soooo good! And you'd pay £30 for that down Toni and Guy's. Don't you love having a hairdresser for a mate?'

How do I get out of this?

Love

Bluegrass

Hey Bluegrass

I've faced something similar so I know how you feel. A friend of mine does colonic irrigation. She used to come over on the weekend, we'd have a couple of ciders, listen to Dick and Dom and then she'd insist on pumping five gallons of water into my lower intestine.*

As a short-term solution, you could do what I did; claim you have a voucher for Charles Worthington's. 'Do they do colonic irrigation there?' my friend asked. 'Not officially', I said, 'but my mum knows the manager and they made an exception.'

But in the long-term you're going to have to do something more serious. Short of pretending you have leukaemia and shaving your head, you might actually have to talk to your friend and explain the situation. You can still have your fun girlie nights in, but just ask her politely to leave your hair alone.

Good luck

Miss Understanding

*Please note this is a fictional anecdote. Nobody pumps *nothing* into Miss Understanding's lower intestine.

Hey thanks for all the great paint name suggestions you sent in.

Blingrrl suggests: Monkey Spew Yellow, Baby Shit Brown and Curry Ring Red.

A bit obvious, if you don't mind me saying?

Grace Harrison has come up with a Goth range and suggests Sombre Black, Undertaker Black, Suicide Black, and Look-Just-Cheer-Up-For-Christ's-Sake Grey.

Jenna Hall likes Pebble Dash Brown, Period Red, Purple Helmet and Chocolate Starfish. Whatever.

My favourite is Fat Gareth's Hard Rock range: Heavy Metal Sheen, Mercury Gloss and Lead Poison.

Miss Understanding Blog Entry
– 22nd May 2010

Blue Sky Corner: Oh God I'm so embarrassed. Marley was up incredibly early this morning making such a damn racket. I got out of bed and marched across the hall, wearing nothing but my see-through vest, knickers and slippers, and I barged into his room to tell him to shut the hell up.

Well he's only got three of his little lunatic friends in there with him, hasn't he? They were playing Buckaroo. Turns out it wasn't as early as I'd thought. Marley wasn't at all fazed but the others looked like they were going to faint. Then the damn horse bucked, flinging plastic all over the place, everyone got a fright and one little boy started crying.

'Er, just keep it down,' I said and beat a retreat. They're *obviously* going to tell their parents. Do you think they'll put me on the sex-offenders register?

Anyway, your Blue Sky challenge this week is to send me your most embarrassing moments, to make me feel like I'm not the only one that does dumb things.

Dad was coming to pick me up around 3.00. I went to find Mum to say goodbye and found her putting on make-up. Mum *never* wears make-up these days. I watched her for a while, remembering what it used to be like, watching her apply eyeliner or smack her lips together trying to smooth out the lipstick. Sometimes, if Dad wasn't around to object, she'd let me put on some rouge or eyeliner.

'What's with the plastering?' I asked, making her jump. 'Is it because Dad's coming?'

'No,' she said quickly, continuing her work, 'I'm going to the theatre.'

'Really? What are you going to see? Ibsen? Chekhov?'

'Marley and I are going to see Bob the Builder.'

'Aha, and the make-up is because you're hoping Spud the Scarecrow will ask for your number?'

She didn't reply.

I picked up a few things on her dressing table, peering at them absently.

'What's this stuff Mum?' I held up a bottle.

'Hmmm?' she looked over. 'Oh, it's a stool softener.'

'Oh. My. God.'

'What do you want, Anya?'

'I just wanted to let you know I'm going back to Clifton this afternoon,' I said.

'OK,' she replied. 'Thank you for telling me.'

Then as I was turning to go, she said, 'Please say a proper goodbye to Marley, won't you? He misses you.'

I can't believe she's playing the emotional blackmail card. That's *my* job.

Back in Clifton, in my peaceful, beautiful room. I borrowed one of Cheryl's crystal healing CDs and am playing it softly through the recessed speakers while I write this, so it'll be a mellow, calming agony column today – my mission is to relax and soothe.

Dear Miss Understanding

I can't stop biting my nails. My mum says that people bite their nails when they're worried about something, and then she says, 'What have you been getting up to, madam?' But like I tell her, I bite my nails when I'm relaxed too. Doesn't matter whether I'm watching *Lost* or *Time Team*, I still taste blood by the second ad-break.

I've tried putting chilli on my fingers, but I accidentally stuck my finger in my eye and it hurt so much I was blinded by my tears, tripped over the cat and fell down the stairs, so I'm not doing that again.

How can I stop?

Geeta

Dear Geeta

Oh boy, do I know how you feel? Did I ever mention before that I have stumps for fingers? I stick a pencil in my gob to type these days. It's not to do with worry, it's to do with the brain-numbing boredom that makes up about eighty per cent of a teenager's life. I could be glib and say, 'Get yourself a hobby,' but you're not nine any more, ladybird farms are all well and good but aren't going to hold your interest for too long.

There are two ways to stop yourself doing it.

1) Stick your fingers up the cat's bottom. The cat won't like it but you'll think twice before nibbling your nails again.*

2) Wear boxing gloves. That way, if your mum keeps giving you a hard time, you can thump her without doing any lasting damage.**

Love

Miss Understanding

*Don't do this.

**Really, don't do this.

Dear Miss Understanding

One of my girlfriend's friends accidentally walked in on me

233

while I was getting changed at her house before Shetta Juhari's Bollywood party and saw my Junior Officer. She was really apologetic and rushed straight out.

Do you think she would have discussed it with the other girls? Might she have told my girlfriend? She didn't mention it but I'm worried because I'm more of a grower than a shower if you know what I mean.

Also, what is a normal size anyway?

Santa

Dear Santa

Why did you call yourself Santa, you cleft? Now I'm going to have nightmares come December about under-endowed Father Christmases doing formation Bangra-dancing with no pants on.

Of *course* she told everyone, you muppet. And the chance that her little visit to see your North Pole was accidental is about as likely as Robbie Williams turning out to be Overlord-in-Chief of some alien invasion force (in other words possible, but unlikely).

Get over it. You ask me if size matters, to be honest I don't know, and I bet she doesn't either. None of us knows anything really.

Sorry,

MU

Dear Miss Understanding,

My girlfriend's heavy into piercing. It started with just a nose ring, which I didn't like so much but she said, 'Do you like it?' and I said yes because I didn't want to hurt her feelings. Then she got a tube thing through her ear, and after that it was a small plate in her eyebrow and then a belly button stud – God knows what she's got further south but I'm not even sure I wanna go there.

Now her face is like a junkyard, with her new fringe she looks like a Transformer.

What can I do, Miss Understanding? I don't want to be snogging Optimus Prime.

Best wishes

Mr Twinky

Dear Mr Twinky

You worked hard to build sympathy during your email, why'd you have to go and throw it all away by calling yourself Mr Twinky? I can't empathize with someone called Mr Twinky. Still, I'm a professional and will try and put it behind me.

I was watching *House* the other day, and they put this patient in an MRI scanner. Well turns out this fool had a piercing somewhere er, intimate, which was ripped out by the powerful magnet, causing a great deal of tissue damage. (I think it ripped a bit of his knob off but they didn't put it into those terms exactly and they speak so *fast* I'm not always sure exactly what's going on.)

Do you have an MRI scanner? No? Well they are available on eBay if you have a spare five grand. But if not, then I suggest you just get over it. If you really like this girl then it shouldn't matter what crap she sticks through her face. If you're not that into her and can't put up with her trying to express her individuality then maybe you're not right for her. Maybe she needs someone who can see past the silverware? Maybe that's why she's wearing it?

Luv

Miss Understanding

Two strange things happened this morning. Dad was at the breakfast table having some toast. I can't remember the last time I saw him eat. He even talked to me.

'Good morning,' he said.

Then before things got out of hand, Cheryl took over. 'Were you planning to go out on Saturday night?'

'Yes, I might go to the Bull, my friend Poops needs a lot of support at the moment,' I said, buttering a bit of toast. Why did she want to know?

'It's just that I thought I might invite Seth over for dinner.'

'Right, well, forget Poops then,' I said. 'But what am I going to wear?'

'Don't worry,' she said. 'I've got that covered.'

We shared a smile.

'See you tonight,' Dad said, 'I'll be late.' He gave Cheryl a peck, me a sort of awkward wave and left. I'd forgotten he'd been there. And now he wasn't any more.

I've had some responses to my plea for your most embarrassing moments. Sarra Clayton wrote in to say:

'Most embarrassing moments: I went to an iPod party. We all had to put the same Playlist on our pods and hit play at the same time so we could all dance to the same song. Well that was all fine until I realized that I'd left mine running all day and I had no battery left so I just jumped up and down like everyone else. It was kind of cool being in that room with no sounds except clumping boots on the floor and a dozen tinny little Jay-Z tracks leaking out of people's headphones but then Shetta Juhari noticed my headphone jack had come out but I was still jumping and so I was busted big time and I was like so shamed I went home.'

Yeah, that's pretty embarrassing. Though I'm with you, Sarra. Jumping up and down is fun even without music.

Bonnie Greaves sent this one in: 'My dad took me to see *The Lion King* a few years ago and we stayed in the Radisson Leicester Square. I got into the lift on my floor to go down to the lobby and immediately noticed this rank smell, like someone had done a massive trouser cough before getting out. I held my breath as the lift went down but it stopped at the sixth floor and who should get on but TV's Alan Hansen!

'Not that I'm all that bothered about what Alan Hansen thinks about me but there's a principle at stake. I said, "It wasn't me."

' "What wasn't y . . ." he started to say before he got a whiff and screwed up his face in disgust. He gave me a look which suggested he was thinking "She who smelled it . . ." Now Alan Hansen thinks I'm a congenital liar who doesn't chew her food properly. That's pretty embarrassing.'

GJ Cole writes in with: 'I'm in Virgin looking for a vintage Patricide album when I come across Paris Hilton's CD single some clown stuck in there by mistake. I pull it out and I'm just shaking my head, when my main crush walks in and sees me checking it out. She just gives me this look like I'm the biggest loser she's ever seen and I'm like, "I'm not into that" but she just booked it. Now I think she's told all her friends I'm into The Hilt. Thank God she didn't see me buy that James Blunt album.'

Email to Al@notmail.com

Hi Al

Thought I should drop you a quick e as I haven't seen you since our lunch date the other week.

Anyway, I had a nice experience at school the other day (and yeah I know that sounds like a contradiction in terms). I was walking down the corridor on the way to Maths, minding my own business as usual when someone yells out, 'Hey, Miss Understanding.'

I couldn't help myself, I looked around to see who it was. It was a girl called Emily Urqhuart, do you know her? She was with her friend Trina something or other, the tall skinny one? Anyway I thought: Uh-oh, this isn't going to end well, so I turned back and kept walking.

'It *is* you,' she said, running after me. 'Anya, isn't it? Anya Buxton? You're Miss Understanding?'

Well I couldn't deny it, so I nodded, wondering if the bullying was going to start here.

But instead she smiled and said, 'I'm Blingrrrl. From your column.'

It didn't click immediately, but then she said, 'You know; one boob bigger than the other, scared of jelly and pigeons?'

'Oh yeah,' I said, 'careful, that'll end up being your epitaph.'

She laughed, so did Trina. Phew.

'Anyway,' Emily said, 'we're going to hang out on the high street after school, though we might check out the new Fat Face. Wanna come?'

I nodded, so pathetically grateful that someone had not only noticed me, but also asked me to do something on a social level, even if it was just looking at clothes I couldn't afford and didn't want anyway.

But then I remembered about having to run for the stupid bus back to Clifton. 'Oh hell,' I said. 'I can't tonight. But maybe some other time? On the weekend maybe? I could come down on Saturday, or Sunday?' I said, sounding needier than a heroin addict on day three at the Priory. Emily didn't seem to notice.

'Sure,' she said. 'Text me on Saturday and we'll hook up.' She gave me her number and suddenly I knew how boys feel.

So I think that means I've got a friend. I've been palibate so long that I've forgotten. But it's a nice feeling.

Cheryl was doing my head in a bit. Going on about this Seth bloke, and how we should get a new dress for when he comes to tea? She wants to take me to London for heaven's sake! Not that I think London's this mythical, terrifying place (which I do a bit) but there's perfectly good dress shops in Wycombe. Or Oxford if necessary. I told her this.

'Oh darling,' she said, 'we won't be going to a *shop*.

We'll be going to a *boutique*. And afterwards I thought we could go to my club. There'll be some dishy young men who'll make Seth look like a tramp with one eye in the middle of his forehead.'

Anyways, drop me a line why don't ya?

Luv

An

Email from <u>Al@notmail.com</u>

Hi An

Funnily enough my dad was asking about you the other day. I think he wants a break from my sisters and is hoping for another snooze in the car. I told him you and I were just friends. 'Oh,' he said. 'I liked that one. Bit too clever for you though.' Nice of him to be so supportive.

Anyway, I was thinking about Cheryl. I know you really like her, and she sounds like good fun, but d'you reckon she sounds a bit too good to be true? Like she wants something from you. Like she wants you to be a younger version of her. A Mini-Cheryl. Cheryl-lite. Cheryl V2.01. Just a thought.

How are you anyway? Are you actually serious about this Seth geezer? He might be a little old, don't you think? Probably has a few girlfriends in London. And The Boy? I really think you're best off without him just now, too. That's my advice anyway.

Got to go and clean my youngest sister's hamster cage (lost a bet). It's all go around here. I'll look for you at lunch tomorrow.

Love

Al

Miss Understanding Blog Entry
– 1st June 2010

Marley's coming over!

I phoned on Monday night and he answered.

'Is Mum there?' I asked.

'No,' he said.

'Where is she?'

'I can't say the word, but it's where you flap your arms about and moo.'

'Ashtanga.'

'Yes.'

'So who's there? Is Lance there?'

'Yes, Mum left some beans for us but Lance said he burned them and had to throw them away but I looked in the bin and they weren't even cooked.'

'So what are you having?'

'Pizza, with *meat*!'

I was warming to Lance.

'Yum,' I said.

'So when can I come?' he asked.

'Hmmm? Oh, right, I said you should come and visit. Erm, how about on the weekend? I'll get Dad to come and collect you on Saturday morning. You could sleep over.'

'Yay!'

'OK, mention it to Mum, won't you? I'll tell Cheryl.'

'OK, bye.' And he hung up. Marley doesn't stand on formality.

'Bye,' I said to the phone.

So I went to see Dad, who was home for once and in his study cutting up bits of cardboard.

'What are you doing?' I asked.

'Building a model,' he replied, not looking at me.

I peered over at his new construction. White lines, white boxes, white trees, white cars.

'Could do with a lick of paint,' I offered.

He sighed. 'I'm working, Anya. Can I help you?'

'Marley's coming over on the weekend, would you be able to pick him up on Saturday morning?'

'Have you checked with Cheryl?' he asked.

I blinked.

'Why do I need to check with Cheryl? He's my brother, and your son. Besides, she won't mind.'

'It's her house too. Check with her,' he said snipping off

a corner of a cardboard square. The little triangular piece landed on my foot. 'If she's OK with it, then I'll collect Marley at 11.00 am sharp.'

Jeez Louise, what's with the etiquette? This isn't *Edwardian Wife Swap*.

So I *did* check with Cheryl. And to be honest, she wasn't exactly enthusiastic. She was out in the garden, on a lounger, looking tiny and beautiful with huge Lindsay Lohan sunglasses on.

'Um, this weekend?' she asked, looking up from her Kathy Lette novel.

'Yes, that's OK isn't it? I'm not expecting you to entertain him. I'll take him down to Clifton and we'll hang about for a bit.'

'And you want to keep him here overnight?'

'Well that makes me sound like a vet, but yes. He can stay in my room.'

I couldn't read her expression behind the glasses, but she gave me a little smile. 'Yes, OK sweetie, he can come.'

'Thanks,' I said, wondering why this was such a big deal.

I phoned Mum and finalized the arrangements. For her part Mum was over the moon. 'He and Lance have been trying to get to the end of *Prince of Persia 5* for about a week now,' she said. 'He's irritable and not eating properly. A break from it will do him good.'

Yeah, I thought, and leave you and Rambling Lance to turn the house into some Hippy Love Shack.

Oh, whatever. Marley's coming. Yay!

Blue Sky Corner: Cheryl's paying for me to go to her gym. We stop by after school twice a week. It's really flash. I used to go to the gym at the leisure centre, which is fine, except for that lady who carries the doll and who's always there staring at you and offering to help you programme the cross-trainer. I thought she was one of the staff for a while, but someone told me she's from the home round the corner and that she doesn't really know how to programme the cross-trainer at all. What's strange about that? No one knows how those buttons work, do they?

This gym is much nicer, it's at the golf course. They have so many courses you can do. I signed up for Tums, Bums and Thighs, but was also tempted by Glute Blast, Circuit Work-it and Body Brick. So that's your challenge for this week. I want to hear your ideas for over-the-top names for really quite humdrum gym classes. I'll write the best ones on a slip and pop them into the suggestion box.

Miss Understanding Blog Entry
– 3rd June 2010

Let me tell you, Cheryl is all over me like a rash at the moment. She's become obsessed with giving me a makeover. I've seen the way she looks at the bottoms of my jeans (the hems at the back that have trailed through mud and rain and unravelled because they're too long) and it's with undisguised disgust. Cheryl wants me in a figure-hugging dress, in strappy heels; she wants my cleavage showing (I'm not entirely convinced I even have one, but she seems confident) and my hair glossier than a *Cosmo* cover. She wants a sleeker, more ladylike stepdaughter, and I'm totally on to her. My mother would have a heart attack, bless her.

Cheryl took me to Knightsbridge (it's in London, duh!) so we could buy me aforementioned tight dress, which she forced me to wear there and then. After that it was lunch at Harvey Nichols, followed by a hideously painful pedicure and manicure.

'Ow,' I'd say as the technician pushed something into my tender flesh.

'Sorry,' she'd reply.

'Ow,' I'd say as she did it again.

'Sorry,' she'd say.

And so on.

They're pretty impressive though, these nails. I could fight crime with them, I felt like I was wearing Marley's Wolverine gloves.

After that it was on to Cheryl's exclusive salon in Mayfair where a bloke with 1970s flicks had the nerve to sneer at my wavy hair before attacking it with GHD irons. Finally I was ejected on to the street looking like a low-grade member of Girls Aloud, while Cheryl dabbed at her unnaturally violet eyes with a tissue.

'I knew you were a swan,' she gushed. 'Underneath all that grunge, I knew there was a swan waiting to show herself off!'

Grunge? What does she mean by grunge?

We ended the day in Cheryl's members club in West London where a handful of posh boys looked down my top and Cheryl pressed drinks on me which, frankly, I had trouble holding on to with my new talons. She introduced me to a few of her friends. Being fifteen years younger than my dad, Cheryl's male friends seemed almost within my grasp – after a few Mohijtos and no dinner, that is. I couldn't understand much of what they were saying but I did remember Cheryl whispering encouraging things into my ear, like; 'Jeremy's very taken with you, darling. Why don't you give him your number?' and 'Isn't this fun?! It's like hanging out with my little sister . . .'

After that I felt very light-headed and slightly ill, and I really wanted to go home. Strangely I kept thinking of my mother's funny wild hair and silly new-age hobbies and shapeless clothes and I wondered what she would make of all this. She'd laugh at it. She'd take the piss. Which is what I wanted to do, but didn't for fear of cracking the pancake make-up. Bloody hell, I thought, do I miss her? That infuriating mother of mine?

I was obviously drunker than I thought . . .

I also had a good look at Cheryl in the back of a cab. You can get away with staring at people when you've had one too many. I have never noticed how much make-up she wears before, or that her mouth can be a little pinched sometimes, or that her hair doesn't move because of all the 'product' in it. She is like a doll. A pretty doll, but . . . maybe just a little bit fake, you know? Like it was all done to impress someone. Someone like me. Maybe Al is on to something here. I'd been right to think that Cheryl is everything Mum isn't. But is that a good thing?

Still, she paid for the ride home and bought us both a Magnum, which was nice of her. Funny thing though, halfway home, when I was feeling more than a little sick from all the sugary drinks and the chocolate I was cramming into my gob like a wasted cookie monster, Cheryl started saying weird things, like, 'Your mother wouldn't take you to London, would she? Your mother probably wouldn't let you wear that dress, would she? She doesn't want you to be attractive, does she? I like having you around, do you like living with us?'

Uh-oh. Could it be that Cheryl wants to be my mummy? But why would she want *me* as a daughter? I'm a total div. Maybe she feels she has to get me to accept her to keep my dad happy? Am I thinking about this too much? I never had to think this hard at home. I mean, at my mum's house. God I'm rambling, must make that appointment with the special doctor.

I don't know, Woodyatt. Am I doing the right thing? Look, please email in with your thoughts. Just what *is* Cheryl's game here? Am I being paranoid? Or does she have some evil twisted plan.

Dear Miss Understanding

I'm going out with this really nice boy, I mean *really* nice. Only thing is, and don't take this the wrong way, but he's a full-on Christian, I didn't realize at first but he kept dropping little hints about forgiveness and virtue and turning cheeks (which at first I thought he was being rude but he so wasn't) then he asked me to go to church with him. I thought it was a nightclub in Oxford so I said yes but he really meant Church church – and not just the local St Andrews but this place like a warehouse down Drummond St with thousands of grinning happy-clappers who all know each other and wouldn't stop smiling at me, like they're hoping for an invitation to my baby shower (after we're married of course).

I like him and he's pretty cute but I'd be lying if I didn't say I was a bit worried about the whole God-squad thing. Am I going to have to have loads of kids and be really cheerful all the time? Cos mornings aren't good for me.

Any advice?

Girdle

Dear Girdle

What is it with Christians? You don't see Muslims walking about smiling all the time, or Sikhs. Bunch of miserable sods, the lot of them – why is it only Christians walk around grinning like the Chuckle Brothers on smack?

Though for balance I should point out that Buddhists can be very smiley.

Look, seriously, you shouldn't judge someone on their religion. I know that sounds obvious, but it's true, think of it this way. What if he was Jewish? Would you be going, 'Hmmm, not sure I want to be hanging about in synagogues washing skull-caps for the rest of my life', or would you be thinking about whether you liked the guy for who he is?

Don't make your decision based on his religion, base it on his opinions. Is he homophobic? Then maybe he's not right for you. Does he want to stone unbelievers? Then he's probably not right for you. Does he want to engineer a clash of civilizations that will slaughter millions and settle once and for all who it is that worships the One True God? Then maybe don't take him round to your parents' to watch the new Richard Dawkins documentary.

On the other hand, does he spend a few hours each week with pleasant, smiley people clapping and singing? Does he do charity work? Does he stop and talk to lots of people he knows on the street?

Then maybe he's OK.

And maybe smiling a little won't kill you.

Your choice

Miss Understanding

Dear Miss Understanding
I've been going out with this guy for a while and I thought I knew him REALLY well but the other weekend we were in my room and I had to go downstairs to help Mum with something. I was gone for about half an hour and when I

came back he looked a bit red-faced and I thought: What's he been up to? Anyway I didn't find out for AGES but when I was going through the photos on my phone I found some pictures of him in my bedroom WEARING MY KNICKERS! I'd thought they were a bit STRETCHED in the front.

Why would he DO THAT? I'm thinking of posting the pictures on the internet to teach him a lesson.

Love

Siobhan

Dear Siobhan

First of all, PLEASE stop SHOUTING at me. I'm not deaf.

Good question though, what's he playing at? Why use your phone camera? Does he think you'll find it sexy? Maybe he gets off on the thought you'll find out. He's certainly got enough issues that some professional should be able to make serious money from. Can I also say that it wasn't actually necessary to email me the pictures? Especially that close-up. I couldn't work out what it was at first, it looked like an anteater wearing a surgical mask.

Look, I kind of feel sorry for the guy, and not just because of the rash. It's NYP though. Not Your Problem.

A) Dump him. Now. By text. Or get a friend to tell him. Or better yet, get a friend to text him.

B) Don't post the pictures on the internet. You may feel

you can justify it by telling yourself you're forcing him out into the open so that he'll get some help, but that's not your call. You can't fix everything and you can't help everybody, I should know. Sometimes the only thing to do is walk away.

Sheesh, some people

Miss Understanding

Great response to my call for OTT gym classes. Here are the best.

Squat Bot! Which sounds a bit like a case of diarrhoea.

Strain Gain Which sounds like someone with the opposite of diarrhoea. To be followed, I'm guessing, by *Groin Strain*. Hahahahaha.

Hero Hour: Wall of Pain Sheesh. Tesco yourself some prune juice already.

Gut Thump I'll pass, thanks.

Pec Success Hmmm . . .

Six-minute Six-Pack Which I might suggest for The Boy, only I think he'd get the wrong end of the stick.

Butt-Crunch For people who've eaten too much dry muesli.

Butt-Blast For people who've eaten too much hot curry.

My fave though is: *Chins, Limbs and Bingo Wings*. That sounds like my kind of class.

* * *

Back in my room. Laptop's screaming for attention. I'll get to your emails in a sec, but for now let me tell you about the Dinner With Seth. Now I thought Cheryl had been going over the top a bit, what with going to London to buy a flash dress and everything. I mean here she is trying to set me up with a gorgeous, loaded bloke. But she's not going to turn me into Tara Palmer Whatserface overnight (I'd need to go on a three-week sick-it-all-back-up diet for starters). She needs to accept the fact that I'm liable to say something embarrassing at any moment, without warning. I can't keep up a pretence of being normal for an entire evening, let alone over the course of a relationship. Wake up Chezza, overdressing me isn't going to help matters.

Now don't get me wrong. I like Seth, and he is bloody gorgeous. I was looking forward to the evening and was a little nervous about seeing him again. But I didn't think there was the remotest possibility he and I might end up together.

Anyway, I didn't think it went too bad, at least to start. Cheryl got me all made up and she twisted my hair up into this pretzel-shape. (At first I said it looked dog-poo shaped and she looked like she was going to strangle me.) We had a glass of cava and talked about boyfriends and it was really fun.

I told her about Al, and how I'd frightened him off by

writing about him on my blog. I was careful not to mention Miss Understanding. Unlike my mother, Cheryl is computer literate and I don't want her nosing through my archive.

'What are you cooking?' I asked. 'Want me to help?'

'Oh darling, I'm not cooking tonight,' she said, laughing. 'I have the caterers in.'

Bloody hell.

She must have seen my look. 'I don't cook much,' she said, shrugging apologetically.

'Fair enough,' I said hurriedly. 'If you can afford catering, then why *would* you cook?'

'Can you cook?' she asked.

'Well. I can pierce a film lid.'

She laughed, then looked all serious. 'Now, when Seth's here, you will be polite, won't you?' she said.

I blinked. What did she care how I behaved?

'I'm always polite,' I said.

She gave me a doubtful look. 'Being polite isn't just waiting for the other person to finish before saying, "yeah, whatever." '

'Do I say that?'

'Sometimes, yes.'

'OK, I'll try,' I said, not at all sure I liked this kind of pressure.

Seth turned up a few minutes early and sat in his car so

as not to ring the doorbell a moment too soon. We watched him out the loo window.

'Gorgeous,' Cheryl said, sighing.

'Yes, it's an XJS convertible,' I told her.

When he finally came in he was all room-filling smiles. He shook hands firmly with Dad, who'd done his time-traveller trick again, seeming to have appeared from nowhere, and having grown a beard.

'Hello, Mr B, it's good to see you again. How's the Edison Conference Centre coming along?'

He kissed Cheryl on both cheeks. 'You look divine, Ches,' he said. 'Thanks for the invite.'

Then he turned to me and almost did a double-take. Had my pretzel come off? But he kept his cool.

'Wow,' he said. 'Really good to see you.'

He slightly emphasized the *really* and the *you*, which made me feel a bit wobbly. He just had such incredible confidence. He was smart, funny, rich and good-looking, and he knew it and just got on with things without being embarrassed about who he was.

We had champagne and minuscule sandwiches in the garden before dinner. The weather was warm again, especially when helped by burning off what was left of the North Sea gas. The bluebells bobbled in the evening breeze.

Cheryl and Seth dominated the conversation, she

peppering him with questions about his mother and his job. He worked in the City, of course, as a trainee broker. Dad and I just sat there sipping our champagne and swallowing sandwiches three at a time. My stomach growled.

'My friend Crumpet's brother works in the City,' I interjected, hoping to elbow my way into the conversation. Cheryl gave me a 'Please Anya?' glare. I think I was supposed to just sit there looking pretty. I tried to sit up straight.

'Really?' Seth said turning to me with a full-beam smile. 'Which firm?'

'I dunno, Something Brothers. Anyway, he told me those brokers get up to some mischief when they let the old hair down.'

'Well, they work hard, and they certainly play hard,' Seth agreed.

'She told me about this game they play, called Spot the Dog,' I went on, ignoring Cheryl, who was clearing her throat in warning.

Seth tried not to smile. 'Oh yes, I think I've heard of that. Remind me of the rules again?'

'It's nearly time for table,' Cheryl interrupted, but I wasn't to be stopped.

'You have to wear white underpants apparently, and drink at least five pints without going for a pee.'

'Uh-huh,' said Seth, encouraging me. 'Go on.'

Cheryl was now giving me the don't-go-there look, and even Dad had started to clear his throat.

'Then you have to do a little wee in your pants then stop quickly, leaving a spot.'

'That's right, I know this one,' Seth said. 'The chap who has the smallest spot wins the game.'

'You do know it,' I said, delighted. 'Do you play?'

'That's classified,' he said. 'What happens in the pub stays in the pub, I'm afraid.'

Dad looked mortified and Cheryl had retreated to her fixed smile. But neither of them could say anything with Seth there.

'I'm hungry,' I said. 'What's for starters?'

Having imposed myself, I quietened down over dinner and just listened to Cheryl yapping at Seth.

Dinner was pretty yummy, I have to admit. The caterers must have cost a bomb. We had a sort of pâté thing with toast for starters, then lamb shanks, then something called spring pudding which was nice but all the raspberry seeds got stuck in my teeth.

'Do you get raspberries in spring?' I asked, trying to get one out from between two molars with the longest of my false nails.

'You do in Guatemala,' Seth said, then realizing he

might have inadvertently offended Cheryl in suggesting she was destroying the planet by demanding Trans-Atlantic punnets, he followed up with, 'Or in poly-tunnels in Cornwall, I believe. These taste Cornish to me.'

'A little tinny?' I said.

Cheryl gave me another despairing look.

'Anya is very on-topic with environmental issues,' she said, 'aren't you, darling?'

'You don't get much of a choice in a house where you're not allowed to use fly spray,' I said.

'Because of the CFCs?' Seth inquired.

'No, because my mum is a giant fly,' I said.

'Anya's mum is very protective towards all forms of life,' Cheryl said, a smirk in her voice.

'Is your mother a bit of a hippy then?' Seth asked innocently.

'What gave it away?' Cheryl responded and laughed a little too loudly. I said nothing, just went back to picking my teeth.

I can't remember what else I said, though I think I may have told everyone The Boy's favourite joke about the factory worker who puts his thingie in the meat slicer. 'Oh my God, what happened?' his wife says. 'I got fired,' he replies. 'No,' she cries, 'I mean what happened with the meat slicer?!' 'Oh, she got fired too,' he says. I laughed more than anyone else, which is embarrassing when it's your joke. I was being a bit silly but I didn't feel like being all sensible and grown up.

Cheryl noticed, of course. After dinner we retired to the lounge, where the caterers served coffee. Dad had two glasses of wine and suddenly remembered how to talk, if not how to be interesting. He chatted to Seth about the beauty of a featureless wall while Cheryl settled down next to me and started whispering.

'I thought you liked Seth,' she said.

'I do. He's charming and attractive.'

'Then why have you been behaving . . . as you have tonight?'

'What do you mean?' I asked innocently, though I knew what she was talking about.

'You've been acting, well a little childishly. All that business with the weeing game and the teeth-picking display. You're usually more sophisticated.'

Sophisticated? I know this is how Cheryl wants to see me, like a middle-class Eliza Doolittle. But it's not who I am.

'Seth's not right for me, Cheryl,' I said gently. 'We're poles apart, and he's too old.'

'He's only just twenty.'

'And I'm only sixteen. He's not going to be interested in a schoolgirl. I know I played up a bit, but he wasn't going to ask me out anyway.'

'Well not now! Honestly, darling, you'll cut off your nose to spite your face.'

Dad and Seth excused themselves and took their glasses of Scotch out into the garden to look at the bricks or something. Cheryl asked the catering for some more Baileys for us and I settled back into the soft couch with my glass resting on my tummy.

'Jugs used to say it was a defence mechanism,' I told her. 'As soon as any boy shows a bit of interest in me I just make myself into this totally objectionable teenager and scare them off. She says it's so I can avoid any kind of commitment.'

'And you know why you do it, don't you?' she said.

I knew what was coming, but asked her to go on anyway.

'It's because of the divorce. Because you saw the pain and anguish it caused. Your parents just stayed together too long, thinking they were doing the right thing.'

Listening to her talk like this made me uncomfortable, even if she is right – and I'm not sure she is. She wasn't the person to be making these comments. She was the main beneficiary of my parents' divorce after all.

She carried on, taking my silence for appreciative contemplation. 'It can't have been healthy for you and Marley to see them argue like that all the time. I told your father he should leave months before he did.'

What?

What?

What had she just said?

She told Dad *months* before? She knew Dad *before*? I sat stunned, trying to run through in my head what I thought I knew about my parents' history. About my *own* history. But then Seth and Dad came back and I wasn't able to ask her any more.

The rest of the evening passed in a haze. The only thing I really remember is Seth kissing me as he was leaving. He passed me his card.

'It was great to meet you properly,' he said. 'Perhaps you'll be in London in a year or so? Please call if you need anything, I know a few people. Or if you want to just hang out, that'd be terrific too.'

And then he left, leaving me a bit nonplussed. Had he just asked me out on a date a year in advance?

After he'd gone, I went back to my bathroom and stood there gawping at myself in the mirror. I did look pretty hot, if I do say so myself. I wasn't sure I looked much like me, but I looked pretty good. As I began the laborious process of scrubbing myself back to normality, Cheryl appeared.

She stood in the doorway giving me a thoughtful look.

'You have a tendency towards self-destruction,' she said.

'What do you mean?'

'You told me you wrote on your blog about your date with that nice boy when he'd asked you not to? You knew it'd drive him away. Why were you being so silly in front of Seth? Were you trying to wind him up? Or me?' She sighed. 'Your actions have consequences you know, Anya.'

Hmmm. I'd forgotten I'd mentioned my blog to Cheryl. Surely she couldn't be reading it, could she? No. She doesn't know the website address for a start. She doesn't know who I am:

Miss Understanding.

Miss Understanding Blog Entry
– 4th June 2010

Thanks for your emails advising me on the Cheryl situation.

Kayleigh Leach says, 'Cheryl wants a baby, it's obvious innit?'

Fat Gareth says that it's my dad who wants a baby, and that Cheryl *doesn't*, so the next best thing is to have me instead. I must say I'd have to be a poor substitute for a baby, though I'm fully toilet-trained and can wipe my own arse much of the time. I think Fat Gareth is wrong.

Guy DuLancey predictably says, 'Cheryl is a total lezzer,' and goes on to make an obscene suggestion. To which I say Cheryl is definitely not a lesbian, and even if she were, I'm not. And even if I were, it would be disgusting and I'm sure illegal to do it with your stepmother. And even if we did it anyway I wouldn't take pictures. And if I did, then I wouldn't show them to you. So *ner*.

So thanks for all those insightful ideas. I'll give them much thought.

Well, I had my first pal-date with Emily and Trina. I think it went well and we've arranged to see each other again next week so it's all good.

We didn't do much really. Just hung about in town. Emily is a phone genius and showed me how to do loads of cool stuff I didn't know about with my Nokia. Only now when it rings it shouts at me: 'Yo bitch, you got yo'self a *call* here!' which I'm not happy with but I can't work out how to change it back.

They asked me about boys and I wasn't sure what to say really. I ended up telling them I was off boys at the moment, which is true I suppose. That whole subject is far too confusing just now. I'll tell you more about that when I've got my head together. Anyway, on to the emails.

Dear Miss Understanding,
I really like those leggings you were wearing on Tuesday, where did you get them?
Luv ya,
Grace

Dear Grace
Grace Harrison yes? The girl who hasn't said one word to

me since September, apart from that time you were standing on my coat at the sports day and I asked you to move and you just grunted at me.

That Grace Harrison? Hmmm, suddenly everyone seems to know who I am. Well, no hard feelings and thanks for your interest, Grace. I can tell you that the leggings came from somewhere over the pond. Cheryl brought them back from NY.

Hang on a sec. This isn't a fashion column. You're supposed to be asking me about personal problems, not suggestions a la mode.

Miss U

PS But thanks for noticing.

Dear Miss U

My boyfriend has a hairy back. Sometimes after we've been cuddling I find I have strands of hair caught in my false nails. What should I do?

Yours

Penny

Dear Penny

Hairy Back? Sounds like a Timberlake track. I dunno, some people like hairy backs. Gives you something to grip on to. When we lived in trees, hairy-backed males had an evolutionary advantage because the baby could cling to the rough pelt as the brute swung through the trees to escape enemies. On the other hand no one wants to get twisty black hairs caught in their false nails. They're expensive, goddamm it!

Be straight with him, ask him to shave, and if he refuses, tie him down and pluck them one by one until he backs down. If you'll excuse the pun.

Yours,

Miss 'Primate' Understanding

Dear Miss Understanding

I've been seeing ghosts. Like that creepy kid in *The Sixth Sense*. All this week outside my house I've been seeing people with really pale faces and blood on their tops. And they're all dressed in old clothes and carrying swords and old-fashioned guns. I think maybe there was a big battle here hundreds of years ago and the ghosts of the dead are forced to fight the battle over and over again for all eternity.

Is there anything I can do to help them find rest?

Yours

Gonk

Dear Gonk

Do you live near Yarrow Common by any chance? Where they've been having those Civil War battle re-enactments for the last week? Anyway, helping damned souls find rest is my speciality. I suggest next time you see one of these ghosts, walk up to him, hold your hand out and say the following Latin words:

Ohyoo palespod

Betchoo dunnow

Owtoo youse dat

Sord, yubatti boy.

And see what happens. Be prepared to run, sometimes ghosts go mental for no apparent reason.

Yours spookily

Miss Understanding

Two things happened after I got home tonight that have really made me think about what I'm doing here. First off, Jugs was waiting for me when I got home. She was sat in the kitchen with a beaming Cheryl.

'Hi,' Jugs said, and rolled her eyes in the general direction of my stepmum.

Cheryl was like an excited puppy, as she always is when she gets the impression I might have some kind of social life. She kept hovering about offering us snacks and drinks. We sat in the kitchen making small talk and waiting for her to get the message that we needed some privacy. Eventually I swiped a couple of Diet Cokes and a bag of Twiglets and the two of us went out into the garden. We avoided the gazebo where the fateful snog had happened.

'So,' I said after opening a can and handing it to her. 'It's good to see you.'

'Yeah,' she said. 'How are you? How's your mum?'

'We're both very well thanks, what about you and yours?'

'We're in good health thanks.'

'Well here's to yours,' I said, clinking her can. Then I sat and looked at her expectantly.

She stared back for a bit. Then eventually she said. 'What?'

'What what?'

'Why are you looking at me like that?' she said.

'Like what?' I said.

'Like I'm expected to open up and tell you everything.'

I shrugged. 'Didn't you come here to talk?'

'No.'

'Well why did you come?'

Now it was her turn to shrug. 'Just to hang out.'

I couldn't believe this. After what she'd done, she just wanted to hang out? My look must have betrayed my feelings.

'Isn't that what friends do?' she said. 'Hang out?'

'No,' I said. 'Well I mean yes, but they do more than that, they talk. They discuss issues. Problems. You know the sort of thing?'

'Actually I don't,' she said. 'What sort of things do you think we should be talking about?'

'Why did you and Poops break up?' I asked.

'I don't want to talk about it,' she said.

I glared at her. 'Was it because he found out you'd been snogging someone else?'

'Are you listening to me?' she said, shaking her head gently. 'I don't want to talk about that.'

'OK,' I said, reasonably. 'Let's talk about what you were doing in that gazebo with The Boy at my party.'

'That?' she said. 'Is that still bothering you?'

My mouth hung open, speechless.

'Anya, you've got to get over that.'

'It'd be a lot easier if you apologized,' I said.

'Well,' she said, 'I'm not going to apologize. What are you going to do about it?'

'I didn't know. I hadn't expected this.

'Are we still friends?' she asked.

'Not if you don't say sorry.'

'Then we're not friends any more,' she said, straight-faced, gulped the last of her drink and stood to leave.

'Wait,' I said, 'we need to talk this over. We can't just end it like this.'

'Yes, we can,' she said. 'Anya, not every problem can be solved with a few trite sentences. Not every problem *needs* to be solved.'

'You're willing to throw away our friendship over a silly snog?' I asked.

'Yes,' she said, 'and apparently so are you.'

And then she left. I sat in the garden for a while and ate all the Twiglets. In a way I felt OK about it. Jugs and I hadn't been getting on for a while. If she didn't want to be friends with me, then fine. I had plenty of friends. Well, I had some friends at least.

As I came in, Cheryl had transformed from happy pixie-creature into foul-tempered hose-beast. Some poor cow at a call centre had cut her off and she really lost her rag.

'I'll get her fired and sent back to her village,' Cheryl screeched at me when she saw me come in. 'Do they still have re-education camps in China?' I watched her ranting and stomping and found myself wondering how Mum would have handled it. For a start, Mum wouldn't have been phoning a call centre in China trying to book a holiday in Barbados (and no I haven't been invited, or at least not yet, I bet the bedtime arguments are ongoing). When we go on holiday we just jump in the Citroen and drive until we get to Gran's house in Devon, or until the car overheats and we have to stop at a Travelodge on the A303, whichever comes first.

Cheryl is fun. We get on famously. I like the makeover sessions and the new dresses. I like her friends and the boys she introduces me to. I'm just not sure her lifestyle is really me, that's all.

Does that sound dumb? It does, doesn't it? It sounds ungrateful and mean. Why am I even thinking like this? I live in a beautiful house, with generous people, I'm near my friends. Oh and that brings me to the second thing that happened this evening. I received a letter from Clifton, accepting me for next term. It's crunch time, sports-fans. What do I do? Do I stay with Dad, his wallet and his caring-but-deranged new wife? Or do I go back to look after Mum and Marley in Bonkers Towers?

Time to turn the tables I think. I'm the one who needs the advice this time.

Miss Not-really-understanding-so-much-any-more

Miss Understanding Blog Entry
– 5th June 2010

Well C to the R to the A to the P. I am gobsmacked. Here are a few emails I received over the last few days.

'Your mum is well mint,' says Gex. 'I wish my child-support worker was more like her.'

'You should be with your mother,' Jenna Hall tells me. 'You need each other. Cheryl's a fruit-loop and your dad doesn't even know who you are.'

Guy DuLancey demonstrates atypical sensitivity when he tells me, 'Get away from The Boy, he's no good for you. You need someone who's giving you respect.'

'Clifton Academy sucks the bigg one,' says Jube. 'Woodyatt is the best 4eva!'

'I love your stories about your mum innit,' writes Bugzapper. 'She's sick, man.'

And even Fat Gareth weighs in with a reminder that, 'Allerton is your home now. You have friends here, as well as family. The people that read your blog live here. We want you to be part of our school, our community. Clifton is lovely, but that part of your life is over now. You're welcome here.'

Fat Gareth. Who knew?

I didn't really expect this, you know. I thought some of you might think I should come to live in Allerton. But I thought there would be loads who'd think I should stay there. I can't think what I've said about Cheryl to make you all dislike her. She's a bit needy, and can be a right moody cow, but still. She's got cupboardsful of accessories and she doesn't mind me borrowing.

I've been thinking about my row with Jugs. About how she said sometimes you can't mend things. Maybe she's right. And maybe I've been trying too hard to mend the big crack between the two parts of my life. Sometimes you must simply make a choice. Though of course sometimes you have that choice taken away from you, as Barrelgirl found.

It's nice that I've got some friends now in Allerton. I like Woodyatt. And Mum and Marley seem to be rubbing along OK. I even like Rambling Lance. Maybe it wouldn't be so bad going back there.

On the other hand there's this room! This huge, stunning, to-die-for room. And my bath! My deep, warm bath. And I can't go back because it would mean packing, and that means opening the cupboard, which I can't do because I would be killed instantly by the falling typewriter. So that settles it.

Dear MU

I have this awful confession, I fancy my best friend's girlfriend and I think she likes me too. She's always giving me these secret smiles and touches me all the time. The other day she comes to my house and the three of us were on the couch watching *Top Hip-Hop* and he goes off to the loo. She puts her head on my shoulder and when he comes back she moves away really quick like she feels guilty.

I think he suspects cos he's been a bit funny with me but I haven't done anything even though I want to. She's well fit, man.

l8rs

Cross Chris

Dear Chris

Oooohhhhhh! Get youuuuu! You're naughty, the ladies can't keep away from Chrriiiissss. You're going straight into the Book of Bad Friends.

Look dude, get over yourself. This sort of thing happens all the time. Whatever you do, don't make the mistake of thinking you are *compelled* to have some clandestine affair with the girl. If you *want* to do that then fine, just get on with it, you don't need my permission. But you don't have to. You have a number of options. To assist, I've drawn up a flow chart:

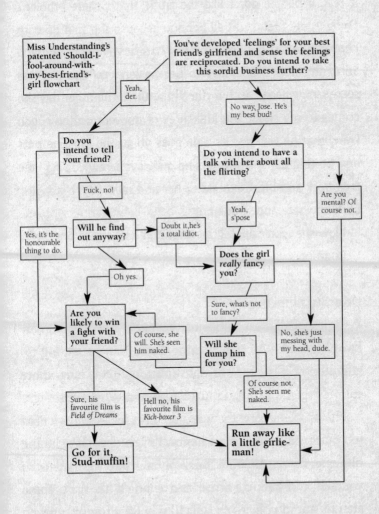

Dear MU

Me had this massive bust-up with me friend, know what I mean? I'm a bit gobby me, I sez what I thinks and I keeping it real. If people don't like the truth, that's there problem. Thing is, my friend was all boohoo because she split up with her bloke to me, but I'm just being honest wiv her to her face. So I turn around and says to her, he left you cos you was always raggin on him man, and she turns round and says to me, naw he weren't you fat slag. So I stood up and says you know that he was and he didn't like your mouth or your fat arse he told me and she gets up and says screw you ho now step back and I turn around to her and says, I ain't stepping back nowhere and so she bugs.

Now she won't apologize, what do I do?

Bugzapper

Dear Bugzapper,

Well first of all, I can't imagine that either of you genuinely have big butts. All that turning around and standing up and stepping back, your conversations must burn more calories than a Chins, Limbs and Bingo Wings class.

The problem here, the way I see it, is that's there's a little too *much* value placed on honesty these days, like it's the ultimate virtue. All these buzz-phrases like 'being true to yourself' and 'keeping it real' and 'telling it like it is'. These are not sound policies on which to build a friendship.

Sometimes the best policy is keeping your fat mouth shut and *not* saying what you think. Sometimes a little white lie is necessary, sometimes a big fat black lie is important. That's how we all rub along together, that's how it all works. I can't imagine living at my house and telling the *whole* truth the *whole* time or even half the time for that matter. I don't want to and no one else wants me to either. People don't thank you for telling them the truth.

And the way you choose to express yourself when you say 'at least I'm honest to her face' is interesting. Why use the words 'at least'? You're justifying telling your friend something you know she doesn't want to hear and you know you're wrong but you've got this stupid moralistic voice telling you that honesty is more important than friendship.

It isn't.

Apologize to your friend and try to work out ways of interacting with the rest of the world without telling it exactly what you think of it 24/7. Maybe the world doesn't need to hear your boring opinion, ever think of that?

Please don't tell me what you really thought of *my* advice, eh?

Lovesy

Miss Understanding

I was revising for Geography last night and looking at an entry on Mozambique. Well, I clicked on vanilla pods, then pod-people, then iPods. Before I knew it I had major Wiki-drift and found myself looking at a video of Apple MD Steve Jobs punching an irate iPhone owner.

So basically I'm going to fail Geography.

I went with Dad to pick up Marley today. He stayed in the car while I went to knock on the door. It felt funny with Dad there. If it had been just me I would have walked in like I owned the place, but I thought I needed to act like a visitor while he was watching, so I rang the doorbell and looked down at the dried mud by the mat that had come off Lance's rambling boots, all punched through with holes, like desiccated waffles.

Mum opened the door and peered over my shoulder, her mouth setting hard when she saw Dad's car.

'Lost your key?' she asked.

I shrugged. 'Didn't want to presume,' I mumbled.

'Don't be weird, Anya, this is your house, come and go as you please.'

I tried not to smile. Then I saw, inside the door, along with Lance's huge size-elevens, was a little pair of Marley-size hiking boots. They looked like they'd been used, too.

Marley came bustling out with a back-pack, munching an apple. 'Bye Mum,' he said and sprinted towards the car. 'Hey Dad!' he yelled, 'I have a mouth ulcer!'

'Seeya,' I said, giving her a smile. She looked happy, I thought. The lines on her face had softened. Getting rid of me and moving Lance in had been good for her. I couldn't come back to live here. It wouldn't be fair on her.

'Bye darling,' she said. And went in.

Email from Al@notmail.com

Hey An

Don't come complaining to me. If you want advice on your problems you should just read back through your own agony columns. Thing is, you never seem to follow your own advice. You can give it out, but you can't take it yourself.

Example: how about when you told Bugzapper that it's OK to lie and fudge and avoid telling the whole truth when it comes to saving a friendship, but when Jugs looked for a reconciliation you were all 'I demand an apology' and 'You betrayed me'. You seemed to be saying that her snogging The Boy was the worst thing in the world, but when Blingrrrl told you she'd snogged someone, and so had her boyfriend, you waved it away and said a quick snog is meaningless.

Also there was that whole Ms Cooper thing. If *you'd* written in to you and said, 'I have some racy photos' – you would have said no. Remember that girl whose boyfriend took photos of himself in her knickers? You told her *not* to put the pictures up. So why did you do it? You told her it was best to sometimes just walk away.

Sorry to get all heavy on you An, but I'm saying you should listen to yourself more. Ask yourself for advice, stop trying to screw yourself up.

Love

Al

PS Just wanted to say I saw you standing on the hockey pitch today, head in the clouds as usual. Someone hit the ball to you and you weren't looking and the other team scored. You didn't even notice. I wonder what you were thinking about? Anyway, I thought you looked very pretty and I like your new haircut. Just wanted to say.

Marley's visit:

It could have gone a lot worse. Nothing went on fire at least. But the house looks like it's been steamed by a gang of hoodies. Cheryl couldn't cope at all. Do you remember those old Tom and Jerry cartoons where the cat chases the mouse around the house and everything gets smashed up? There's always some lady who screams and gets up on a chair to get away from the chaos, well Cheryl was like that. She'd just stand there going, 'Marley, could you put that lamp down?' or 'That's lovely darling, but that tennis racket is rather expensive,' or 'Anya could you perhaps suggest to him he doesn't eat the potpourri?'

Dad didn't come out of his study at all. I think he may have climbed out the window and legged it back to his office in London.

For his part Marley had a ball, and I enjoyed it too, though I'd forgotten how tiring looking after a six-year-old could be. I took him down to the village to give Cheryl a break for a while. We wandered about the three shops, went to look at the water wheel and realized we'd exhausted the entertainment possibilities of Clifton. Then Marley nearly got us arrested by picking the flowers on the green. We beat a hasty retreat and headed back to the house.

'They're for Cherry,' he said, which was what he'd decided she was called. 'She's very pretty.'

'She is pretty,' I agreed.

'Not as pretty as Mummy,' he said accusingly.

'Er, I suppose Mummy has a certain . . . quality.'

'Not as pretty as you either,' he said. 'Here you can have this.' He handed me a length of clematis he'd ripped from the side of the bandstand.

'Thanks Marley,' I said. 'So, do you miss living in Clifton?'

He shrugged. 'I like it in Allerton, there's more to do. And I like Lance.'

'Yes, he is nice isn't he? Is he around a lot then?'

'Sometimes, but sometimes him and Mum argue and

then he doesn't come around for a bit.'

'Do they argue a lot?' I asked, concerned.

'Mum does,' he said. 'Lance just makes faces at me behind her back and tries to make me laugh.'

I'm liking Lance more and more.

As we came in, we saw Cheryl standing pretty much where we'd left her, looking horrified at the mess. I took Marley straight into my bedroom, where he immediately opened the cupboard and was nearly crushed by the torrent of crap that leaped out at him.

We played board games and I read him stories. After what seemed like months, it was dinner time. Cheryl watched him in astonishment as he devoured an entire packet of sausages and a huge plateful of chips and baked beans.

'He doesn't normally get to eat food like this,' I explained. 'He's gorging.'

'What does your mother usually give him?'

'Brown stuff,' Marley said through a mouthful of beans.

'Lentils, brown bread, wholewheat pasta, tofu, quorn. That sort of thing,' I explained.

Cheryl sniffed. 'Poor little fella,' she muttered under her breath. I suddenly felt defensive.

'He's healthy enough, loads of energy, anyway.'

She shrugged and nodded. 'Are all children like him?' she asked.

'Not exactly like him,' I said, watching as he took a bite out of a sausage-and-chip sandwich he'd made.

We finally got him into bed and Cheryl had to read him a story. I was in the bathroom exfoliating and listening to Marley berating her for not telling the story properly.

'You missed a page,' he cried. 'You didn't read the bit where the goblin farts on the princess.'

Afterwards, we sat on the couch and she had a large glass of wine. I had a cup of hot chocolate.

'How do you do it?' she asked.

'How does my mother do it, you mean?' I said. 'I don't know, she makes it seem easy.'

I was starting to appreciate just how much Mum did for Marley when I wasn't around. And starting to understand why she asked me for help when I was.

'Oh well, you don't have to worry about that sort of thing any more, not now you're here,' she said, finishing her wine. She stood. 'Sure you don't want one?' she asked waggling her glass. I shook my head. I was also starting to understand why the recycling box out the front of my mum's house was always full of wine bottles.

Cheryl was right I guess. Marley wasn't my problem any more.

Miss Understanding Blog Entry
– 22nd June 2010

I *know*, OK. Stop emailing me to tell me I haven't done much of the agony thing for a while. It may have escaped your notice but I've got problems of my own at present. If there's to be any self-indulgent whining around here it'll be done by moi, capisci?

Went down to the Bull tonight. Saw Poops there, with a girl. I just stood there at the bar, not sure whether I should go and say hi or what. Eventually he saw me and waved me over.

'Hi,' he said. 'This is Lauren.'

She half smiled at me, presumably wondering if I was an ex she should hate, or even worse, Poop's BFF, in which case she'd need to destroy me utterly. The only thing worse than an ex your boyfriend still hangs out with, is a BFF he's never slept with, cos he'll have something with her you can't replace, and you can't make him stop seeing her without revealing your inner hose-beast.

'Hi Lauren,' I said brightly, wondering if I should sit down. Normally by now Poop would have bought me a drink.

'How are you?' he said.

'Oh I have a slight brain haemorrhage,' I said, 'but I've taken an Anadin Forte so I'm sure it'll clear up.'

Lauren looked at me as if I were insane. Poops spoke up.

'Oh Anya does this thing where she pretends to be sick the whole time,' he said.

Not any more she doesn't, I thought. That little bit of fun seems to be over.

'It's really funny,' he told her, forgetting that if you have to explain it, it isn't funny. She smiled thinly. Then I was saved, I saw Jake and Crumpet over the other side of the pub.

'Anyway,' I said. 'I'm gonna pop over there for a bit. I'll see you cats later.'

Poops looked relieved, Lauren delighted.

I got myself a half of shandy and went to join the others.

'Hey what's with Poopgelina over there?' I said. 'How long have they been going out?'

Jake shrugged. 'Since your party.'

287

I blinked. 'She was at my party?'

'No, she was at the pub we all went to when Cheryl the Peril kicked us out.'

'I didn't know you went to a pub,' I said, a little sniffily. 'Any other romances I should know about?'

They looked at each other quickly, and then I realized. Crumpet looked a little embarrassed. Jake looked pleased with himself.

'Oh, OK,' I said. 'I mean that's brilliant. I'm so happy for you guys. Why didn't you tell me?'

Crumpet shrugged. 'It's not as if you send an e-nouncement for this sort of thing – anyway, we weren't sure how you'd take it.'

'What do you mean?'

'Oh nothing,' she said too quickly. 'We just didn't want to let it all out too early.'

I sat back in my chair, realizing what she was getting at. 'Ah, you mean you didn't want me to put it on the blog.'

'Yeah kind of,' she said. 'Sorry.'

'That's OK,' I said again. 'I understand.'

Talk about out of the frying pan into the chip pan, I now wish I'd stayed with Poops and Lauren Thin-Smile. I excused myself and went to the loo. I had one last hope. I phoned The Boy. For once, he answered.

'Hey,' he said, 'where are you?'

* * *

I took a cab to the Cricketers. The Boy had a licence and a car of sorts, but he had nine points on his licence and no petrol in his car. So I took a cab. We sat outside, so he could smoke and so I could watch him smoke and tut at him. He'd shaved for once and he almost looked respectable. 'Court appearance tomorrow?' I asked.

'Job interview,' he replied.

I snorted. 'Not dog-walker again? They never did manage to fish that cocker spaniel out of the storm drain.'

'Actually it's a decent job,' he said, affronted. 'With prospects.'

'Sorry, what is it, local vicar? Bank manager?'

'Forklift driver at the Asda Distribution Centre,' he said.

'I didn't know you could drive a forklift.'

He shrugged. 'How hard can it be?'

'So you *can't* drive a forklift. Well, good luck.'

'Thanks.'

'What about the demo tape?' I asked. 'Did you send it to anyone?'

'It's not going to happen,' he said. 'I've given up dreaming about that.'

'OK, but don't give up your forklift dreams now, will you? That *would* be a crime.'

He came around and sat on my side of the table, looking into my eyes. 'You're really beautiful, you know that?'

How is it that boys can do that? Make you melt with just a few simple words? Just seconds before I'd been shaking my head in despair and amusement at how hopeless this guy was, then all of a sudden he pays me a compliment he probably doesn't even mean and I immediately find myself wanting to have his children and to pay for him to record an album full of dumb songs I hadn't even heard yet. Then he leaned forward to kiss me. And I did practically the hardest thing I've ever done.

I turned my head.

He sat back and stared at me in surprise. I stared back, trying to look like the ice-queen I wanted to be.

'OK,' he said, 'talk about misunderstandings. When you said you were coming over I thought . . .'

'You were right,' I said, 'but I've changed my mind.'

'Is it the forklift thing?'

I laughed. 'No.'

'It's the music, isn't it? You think I should have these fantasies about becoming a rock god. You think the fantasies are important.'

I shrugged. 'Dreams *are* important,' I said.

'Not dreams,' he said. 'Fantasies. It's not going to happen, Anya. I'm not going to be a musician. Understanding the difference between fantasies and reality, that's important.'

'Knowing the difference between a two-way- and a

four-way-entry Europallet is important too, I suppose,' I said.

'Eh?'

'Anyway, that's not it,' I said. 'I'm not saying no to you because of you, I'm saying it because of me.'

'It's not me, it's you? Is that it?' he said, smiling.

'Yeah something like that. And while we're on the clichés, I feel like I need some space to find myself.'

'Uh-huh,' he said, sipping his beer.

'Thing is,' I went on. 'I came back to Clifton to try and get something back, when I'm not sure it was here in the first place.'

'I never promised anything, Anya,' he said.

'No I don't mean you, or at least not *just* you. After we moved to Allerton and I found myself so miserable, I think I made up this picture of myself living this happy life back here, surrounded by friends, and boys, all smiles and happy families. And it wasn't really like that. I didn't really fit in here any more than I do in Allerton, and now I realize that I quite like it that way. I don't need friends, they let you down, or you let them down. It's good to have someone to have a drink with on a Friday night, but that's all really.' I touched his arm. 'In fact you've been the only consistent person in my life lately. Consistently unreliable, that is. Quite endearing in a way.'

He looked hurt, but didn't deny it.

'I'd better go,' I said. He looked like he was about to say don't, but stopped himself just in time. The Boy doesn't beg, after all.

As I walked off though, he called out, 'Hey, Little Miss Understanding.'

I stopped.

'When you're a famous author, could you put in a good word for me?' he called, across the beer garden, while the regulars pretended they couldn't hear.

I turned and smiled. 'Sure,' I said. 'Why not?'

Like that's ever going to happen.

Email to Al@notmail.com

Hey Al

Such a strange thing just happened. I was lying on my bed just now, staring at the ceiling, listening to Brendan Benson and wondering how long it had been since I saw my dad, when I had a thought. Dad had said I should come to see his offices in London. Maybe it was time to take him up on that offer. I had a few things I wanted to ask him about. I went to find Cheryl to ask if she had his work email. I checked the sitting room, then the garden – no luck. She wasn't in the kitchen or her bedroom. Her car was still here so she must have still been in the house. I wandered up the stairs and heard tapping coming from the study.

I hate it when people interrupt you just as you're in the middle of a brilliant sentence so I stood in the doorway and waited for her to stop. As she typed I couldn't help but look at the screen. It looked very familiar.

Without thinking, I found myself moving forwards, trying to get a better look, until I found myself standing right behind her as her ridiculously long nails clattered madly against the keys of the Dell. On the screen, behind Cheryl's email window, but clearly visible was my website.

I didn't know what to do; I thought about clearing my throat, but wasn't sure I wanted to confront her about it just then. I desperately wanted to read the email she was writing, but forced myself not to. Instead I softly walked backwards and out of the room, trying to figure out what this meant.

I came back down to my room. So she *was* reading the blog. How had she found it? Had one of my friends told her, at the party? My mother certainly wouldn't have done so. The only other people who knew were the school. And then it hit me, the letter they'd sent to Dad. She'd intercepted it, like she intercepted all his 'household mail'.

Do you realize what this means Al? She's been reading everything I've been saying about her, and Dad, and this house, and my doubts over my life. When I wrote all that stuff I didn't expect anyone . . . you know, grown up to read it. It was just supposed to be for us. For us teenagers.

I feel violated. How dare she?

Anyway, I phoned Dad and told him I was coming to London and could we meet for lunch? He didn't sound keen but I kind of insisted. He's not good at saying no really. Not sure I want to write about it on the blog, so I'll email you later, OK?

Luvs

Anya

Email to <u>Al@notmail.com</u>

Me again, on the way home. This is what happened:

I stood at the foot of the most boring building I've ever seen. I think Alan Sugar owns it. It's slap-bang in the middle of Docklands, and even though it's thirty storeys high you just don't notice it. The other buildings around it say, 'Hey Anya, look at me, I'm big. I'm strong. I can reflect the sun into your eyes. Look at me!' These are the sort of buildings Alan Sugar likes to *pretend* he owns. He probably sits inside his building, thinking: This building is really crap. Not like those buildings, they're cool. I wish I owned those buildings.

Dad's building just says *27 Limehouse Rd* on it in big, boring letters. I went into reception and told them my dad was expecting me. The fat man behind the counter stared at me in astonishment, as though no one had ever come into the building and asked to see someone before. I wandered about the reception area as I waited, all the while thinking: Please don't let me work in a place like this . . . Please don't let me work in a place like this . . .

Against his better judgement, the fat man phoned Dad and raised his eyebrows when he got the response.

'You can go up,' he said. 'Fifteenth floor.'

'Thanks,' I said, as cheerily as I could manage, and hopped into the lift.

Dad greeted me on his floor. He seemed quite pleased to see me. I think my visit may turn out to have been the most interesting thing to happen there for years. Dad walked me down to his office, and dozens of pairs of eyes turned to watch me pass. I turned my head quickly to catch them but they all looked away just in time.

I went into Dad's office and walked to the window. Unlike the reception area, the view was stunning. I stared out over the East End, towards the Barbican. To my left I could see a long, graceful sweep of the river, silver in the haze.

'How do you get any work done, with this view?' I asked.

'Hmmm?' he said, tidying up some documents on his desk. 'I don't notice it any more. I usually have the blinds closed, but the cleaner was in this morning.'

'Let's go to lunch,' I said, rolling my eyes.

We went to Carluccio's and I had *orecchietti con pesto*. Dad asked me if I wanted any wine. I think he's concerned about how much I drink. 'Just sparkling water please,' I said primly.

'Ready for your . . . exams?' he asked, obviously trying to remember where I was in the school calendar.

'Yes,' I said. 'Dad, can I ask you a question?'

'Of course,' he said, probably expecting something about walls, or bricks.

'How long had you been seeing Cheryl before the divorce?'

He stared at his glass for a long time. He wasn't used to having to deal with questions like this.

'A while,' he said, eventually.

'Did you want another baby?' I asked. 'Was Mum too old?'

His brow furrowed, and for the first time in years, I saw he was angry.

'That's none of your business, Anya,' he said. 'I'm not proud of what happened, I didn't handle it well and I'm sorry for my part in the split. But I'm not going to sit here and trawl through the . . . the history of it all just to satisfy your curiosity.'

I sat and watched him, hoping for more.

'It's over, Anya, we've all moved on. Please let it go.'

'Look,' I said. 'Just answer one question, was Mum drunk that night?'

He sighed. After some thought, he said, 'The problem with that is that if I answer that question I'll have to explain so much more. It's not a fair question.'

'So that's a yes then,' I said.

'Yes,' he agreed, reluctantly, 'but there was a reason she was drunk.' He paused.

'Go on,' I said.

'She'd been at a restaurant, with a friend. Her friend had driven them there.'

I shrugged. 'And?'

'And while they were there, her friend told her that I was having an affair.'

I nodded, now it was clearer. 'So Mum went mental, grabbed this lady's keys and drove off to come and find you.'

He nodded. 'Yes, exactly. Your mother isn't normally so irresponsible, she was furious and not thinking straight.'

'I can imagine,' I said. 'Poor Mum.'

'Yes,' he said. 'Poor Jocasta.'

Then it hit me. I thought it through a few times, trying to figure it out.

'Erm,' I said. 'One thing, though . . .'

He waited, knowing what was coming.

'You said Mum's friend had driven her. But Mum

was driving your car when she crashed. How does that work exactly?'

He said nothing.

'Who is this "friend" of Mum's?' I asked.

To his credit he looked me square in the eyes as he answered.

'Cheryl. It was Cheryl.'

'I see,' I said, not really seeing it at all. 'So Mum and Cheryl were friends before?'

'Yes,' he said. 'You see Cheryl worked for my firm, this firm. She was my PA for years. When your mother used to call for me and find I was busy, she would chat to Cheryl for ages – they became close. Your mother used to joke that Cheryl was my work wife.'

I winced.

'I know,' he said. 'I told you I'm not proud of what I did.'

'So let me guess,' I said, 'you couldn't bring yourself to tell Mum about the affair, so Cheryl did it instead.'

He nodded.

'OK,' I said. 'That's it. I've heard enough.'

His face took on a look of immense gratitude.

Then to change the subject as much as anything, I said, 'Look Dad, I'm thinking of moving back to Mum's.'

He rolled his eyes. 'For heaven's sake.. Because you found out about Cheryl and me?'

'No,' I replied. 'Because I think Mum needs me.'

He frowned at me. 'You must do what you want, Anya, but you can't go on changing your mind the whole time. You can't live in both places. You have to make a final choice.'

'I know,' I said.

'Cheryl loves having you around, you know?' he said.

'And you Dad? What about you?'

'Think about her too, won't you?' he said, ignoring the question. 'She gets lonely in that house, it's good that you're there for her.'

So is that what I am? Cheryl's companion? Am I to live there for ever? Growing old with her, making her tea and helping her with her jigsaws?

I nodded and pushed my plate away. I'd got what I came for. We finished the meal in silence. I kissed him on the cheek outside the restaurant and walked off towards the river. I needed to clear my head and think things through. I'm not sure I'm really that horrified that Dad was cheating on Mum for so long before they split. There was obviously a big problem there. And maybe it is all for the best. But they could have told me.

They could have bloody well told me.

Miss Understanding Blog Entry
– 25th June 2010

I came in through the front door as someone had locked the side gate. As I opened it a wave of dirty brown water came sloshing out and soaked my feet. I sighed, thinking Mum must have left the bath running again. But it was worse than that. The entire ground floor was flooded. I sloshed my way through various rooms. Furniture had been rearranged into piles. I heard a banging noise in the kitchen and went through to find Marley there wearing oversized goggles and nailing a breadboard to an upturned table.

'What are you doing?' I asked. He looked up from his work, expressing no surprise at my sudden appearance.

'Building a raft,' he said, as if this should have been obvious. 'It's getting deeper and I want to be able to float up the stairs.'

'OK,' I said, evenly, trying not to scream. 'Er, where's Mum?'

'In the tent,' he said. He nodded towards the open back door.

I splashed outside and took off my shoes so as not to muddy the lawn. Mum had put her Glastonbury tent up in the garden. If there is one thing Mum is good at it's putting up tents. From bivouacking in Africa, to establishing a tent-city outside a US air force base, there is nothing you can teach Mum about pegs, groundsheets and holes in the ground for doing your business in.

I walked into the tent to see her sitting cross-legged and reading her Tom Cruise autobiography, it was by now a little damp and she still hadn't got very far into it. I'm really not sure she's right for Scientology. She doesn't watch films, hates sci-fi and has no money. She was wearing a garish, multicoloured jumper, obviously hand-knitted by her or one of her knitting-club weirdos.

'Does Noel Edmonds know you're wearing his jumper?' I asked.

She started and looked at me as if I were a ghost. She stared for a good long time, trying to figure out what this meant. Eventually she asked, 'Do you know anything about stopcocks?'

'I don't know anything about any sort of cocks, to be honest with you, Mum. Now, if only we knew someone who was going out with a plumber . . .'

'We had a row,' she said and shrugged meekly.

'And this is his revenge?'

'No, it's just that he was halfway through fixing something when it all went wrong.'

'Oh,' I said, sitting down on a quilted yak-hair pillow, which I immediately regretted as the bristly hairs of the long-dead yak jabbed me up the backside vengefully. It was lovely and warm in the tent. I felt dreadfully tired. I just wanted to curl up on the cushions for a bit.

'How long are you here for?' she asked, tentatively.

Suddenly it was all a bit much and I started crying. She leaned over and hugged me, her technicolour jumper now not seeming quite so silly. It was some time before I was able to get out the words: 'I'm here for good Mum. If you'll have me.'

'As far as I'm concerned, you never left, darling,' she said.

Tell you what, natural wool is lovely and soft. I buried my head into half a sheep's worth of softness and warmth and tried to stop crying.

'I'm sorry,' I sobbed. 'I've been a brat.'

'It's OK,' she said rocking me gently. 'I've been a little childish myself, I can see that.'

'Sometimes we all need to be a little childish,' I said. 'I quite like it when you're silly, Mum.'

'Yes, but sometimes we need to be grown up too,' she said. 'I know I can do better at that.'

302

I squeezed her tightly and listened to the baby blackbirds rustling and chirping in the hedge behind the tent. Somewhere in the distance Marley was still hammering away at his raft.

'I liked that CD you made me,' Mum said. 'The one you gave me for Christmas.'

She was lying, but I appreciated the sentiment. 'And I liked the yoga mat,' I said, though I had no idea where it was.

'Oh, and another thing,' Mum said. 'I've relaxed the meat ban. Marley and Lance ganged up on me.' This was excellent news.

'Can't say I missed your Tofu Surprise,' I admitted.

'Well there's some dead cow in the freezer,' she said. 'It was surprisingly cheap.'

'You make it sound so appetizing. Can we have it with quinoa?'

'I've run out of the gluten-free.'

I sighed. 'Sometimes you just have to take a chance.'

Email to: Cheryl73@notmail.com

Dear Cheryl

I know you've been reading my blog. I don't mind. I wish you'd told me, but I don't mind. I just wanted to let you know why I've decided to move back to Allerton. To live with Mum. Please don't take it the wrong way. I really loved living with you and Dad, we had a laugh. I know I've said some mean-sounding things about you on this blog but I write mean things about everyone, I hope you understand that. I genuinely think you're a kind, warm and funny person.

I was surprised to read some of the negative things that my readers wrote about you. I'd hate to think that they'd only picked up the negative parts of your character that I'd mentioned. I should have spent more time expressing how much you made me laugh, how kind you were to welcome me into your house and how good your late-night hot chocolate is.

Oh and also how good you are for my dad. Maybe that's the most important thing of all.

I couldn't figure out at first whether you were trying to be my new mum, or my new best friend. I'm still not sure but I like you best as a friend. I already have a mum. I hope we can still be friends.

Lots of love

Anya

XX

PS Oh BTW – when you open the cupboard in my room, you need to stand well back and use the broom handle.

Turns out that stopcocks are basically just taps in

cupboards. Usually under the sink. Lance explained what I needed to do over the phone. He said the water should drain away on its own in a day or so, then we could get started on the clean-up.

'And are you going to be involved in this?' I asked. 'I'm sure Mum would like to see you.'

He sighed heavily, like a man on Death Row whose lawyer has just said, 'Don't worry, we can always appeal again.'

'She can be a little difficult sometimes,' he said.

'Yes, but that's part of her charm,' I said. 'Difficult people are the most interesting.'

'Only to advice columnists,' he said.

'And plumbers,' I countered, though I wasn't quite sure how that worked.

He didn't say anything, so I played my ace.

'Marley misses you.'

'Oh Anya, that's not fair,' he said. 'Don't give me that father-figure thing.'

'I'm not,' I said firmly. 'It's not a case of you replacing Dad, things aren't ever that simple. I understand that. You're not Dad, or Dad Mark Two. You're just Lance. Rambling Lance.'

'Thanks,' he said flatly.

'Rambling Lance the Welsh Goat-man,' I continued, as usual not knowing when to stop.

'Yes thank you, Anya,' he said. 'OK, I'll pop around tonight after work. I can check your mum's pipes at least.'

'I really hope that's not some kind of euphemism,' I said.

He laughed, and I knew I had him then. Marley walked in at that moment, and went down on his arse when he stood on a pipe which rolled out from under his feet.

'We really miss you round here,' I said.

'Is that Lance?' Marley asked excitedly. 'Ask him if he has a snorkel.'

After we'd got Marley into bed, still wearing his goggles, Mum and I settled down on the couch and watched Five US on Mum's new flat screen.

'Did Dad want another baby?' I said, out of the blue. 'Is that why he went off with Cheryl?'

Mum didn't seem surprised at my forward question. It was as if she understood the new deal. That I wanted to know more about her and why she was the way she was.

'No,' she replied. 'I wanted another baby. He didn't.'

'Are you sure he didn't?'

'Just look at the car he bought himself. You can't fit a baby seat in an Audi TT.'

That was true.

'It's just that I got the impression Cheryl . . .'

'Go on,' she said, giving me permission to talk about the Housekeeper.

'I just thought maybe she was keen to have a child.'

'Why, because she was fawning over you?'

'Yes,' I said. 'How did you know?'

She shrugged and got up, walked to the kitchen and came back with a bar of dark chocolate. She snapped it neatly in half and handed my bit to me before sitting down again.

'The thing about the Housekeeper . . . about Cheryl,' she said, 'is that she's insecure. She's quite a sad person really. She wants to be young and beautiful and she likes having the money and the house and the experience that your father has now.' There was a brief pause while she munched on a square of chocolate. 'But I think she's a little regretful that she doesn't have the other bits too, that she didn't get to share in the life your father has already led. The family, the kids, the memories. I'm sure it isn't conscious, but perhaps deep down she feels that by getting closer to you, she's a part of that.'

'She's jealous of you. Jealous of us?' I asked, as she stopped talking to lick her fingers.

'Well you could call it jealousy, or maybe regret.'

Mum then laughed at some lame joke on the sit-com we were watching. I sat and thought this over. It made sense.

'Poor Cheryl,' I said.

'Hmph,' Mum said. 'Don't go overboard, she's still a home-wrecker.'

I thought about it for a bit. 'She's not a bad person though,' I said.

Mum was silent for a while. Then sighed. 'No, I suppose she has her good points. I know everything's not black and white, Anya. People aren't defined by just one characteristic. Cheryl may have been looking for a mini-Cheryl when she agreed to let you live with them, but I think she grew to like you for who you are. I rather think that's something Miss Understanding might have learned this year.'

There was a thirty-second period in which neither of us said anything. The only sounds were some crappy mobile-phone ad blaring out of the telly . . . and my beating heart.

'You *have* been reading my blog then?' I asked finally.

'I've been dipping in,' she confirmed.

'That's how you know so much about my relationship with Cheryl?'

'Yup.'

'Mum!'

'Well, you never phoned,' she said defensively. 'I wanted to know what you were up to.'

'Is nothing private?' I protested.

'Not the bits you put on the internet,' she said calmly.

'Stop being so . . . logical,' I said.

'I don't mind, Anya,' she said. 'I like it. I like how you write me.'

'You *do*?' I asked, incredulous.

'Yes, I'm not really like that, of course.'

'Yes, you are.'

'No, I'm not.'

'OK *what*-ever.'

Email to <u>Poops@notmail.com, Jugs@notmail.com,</u>
<u>Crumpet@notmail.com, Jake@notmail.com</u>

Hi Guys

1) Sorry

2) Sorry

3) Sorry

4) Really sorry

Sorry number one is to Poops for never buying you a drink – promise I'll buy all the rounds next time I come back to visit.

Sorry number two is to Jake for using your real name on the blog and getting you into trouble with your mum when someone told her you were involved in the Great Boots Window Caper.

Sorry number three is to Crumpet for being so self-obsessed I never even thought to ask how you were doing or *who* you were doing.

And sorry number four is to Jugs for asking you to say sorry when there was nothing to say sorry for. At all.

I know I've been a crap friend lately, guys, and I promise things are going to change. I'm not going to talk about you on the blog any more. Maybe we could all arrange to meet up at the Bull. And I'm not going to interfere in anything or ask any questions or talk about things that you don't want to discuss. And if The Boy turns up someone else can sit on his knee.

Love you all, write soon

An

Miss Understanding Blog Entry
– 30th June 2010

I was rudely awakened this morning by a six-year-old superhero with eggy breath. It's good to be back. But as I was munching on gluten-free toast downstairs, I suddenly remembered I haven't magically solved all of your problems with a few deft clichés for ages. You guys must be a *mess*, I thought. I came up to the laptop and sat for a bit. Then I deleted my inbox.

You know what, Woodyatt? I'm gonna take a little holiday. I need a break from all this. I need some time to get my head straight. I realized all this time I've been dispensing advice to you losers, and it turns out I'm the biggest loser of them all. Who am I to tell you how to live your lives? What the hell do I know about it?

And another thing, I've been spending far too long hunched over this laptop, like some wizened crone – except with good teeth and high cheekbones. I'm turning into a mouse potato. In fact I'm off into town later to catch up with Em and Trina – we're going to hit Superdrug and give each other thirty-second makeovers with the testers.

But I promise you one thing. After the exams, after the hols, after I get my shit together, I'll definitely be back. Maybe doing the agony thing, maybe something else. But I'll be back. You'd better believe it.

And just before I sign off, one last email from someone who's nearly as big a loser as me.

MU

Dear Miss Understanding

I had this date last night with a girl who writes an agony column. We dated a while ago, then we were just friends, but now I think I want something more and I think maybe she does too, though she's impossible to read. I think the date went really well to start with. We went to Pizza Express and shared some garlic bread. She seemed to laugh at my jokes, even the one about the French exchange student and the tube of Pringles, which, in hindsight I appreciate wasn't at all appropriate.

We saw *Stomp Da Yard 4*, which I pretended to want to see, and she seemed to enjoy it hugely and was sort of doing the dance moves in her chair and whacked me a nasty one with her elbow at one point. She offered me some popcorn, which I accepted and this seemed to enrage her, so I didn't have any more. Then afterwards I walked her home and I thought she wanted me to kiss her when we got to her house and so I sort of moved forward and then she sort of turned away so I stopped, but then it was like she'd realized what I was trying to do, so she stopped and moved back towards me but by then I'd pulled away and it all got totally awkward and I didn't know what to do so I just held out my hand and she looked at it and eventually shook it and was looking at me like I'm the biggest butt-munch on the planet and I was so embarrassed I said g'bye really quickly and legged it.

So I'm sure that now she thinks I'm a total idiot and rude as well, and I just wondered how you thought I should go about letting this girl know that I really like her and that I'm sorry for being a div and would she like to go out with me again and I promise I'll properly lunge at her if she gives the remotest suggestion she might like a kiss at the end.

Your thoughts?

Al

Dear Al

Gosh, is this the same girl you wrote to me about before? Because this one seems even more amazing than the last. You sure try to punch above your weight, don't you?

Sounds like the date went OK, though you have to be careful not to pretend too hard to like chick-flicks because some girls worry if their date is genuinely into that kind of thing.

Also sounds like you did screw up the bit at the end. It seems to me this girl was giving out clear signals that a chaste peck on the cheek might not be met with a slap, you had to turn it into some kind of hip-hop routine.

You need to sort that out, OK? Don't be nervous. I think she might like you, though I also think she probably hasn't really decided yet and is still narked about the popcorn incident.

Either way, you should definitely ask her out again next weekend. Who knows where it will end up?

Twinkles!

Miss Understanding